A MAINE CHRISTMAS... OR TWO

A DUET:
THE BILLIONAIRE'S ANGEL &
A MERMAID ISLE CHRISTMAS

J. S. SCOTT & CALI MACKAY

A Maine Christmas...or Two

ISBN: 978-1-939962-39-3 (E-Book)

ISBN: 978-1-939962-40-9 (Paperback)

Cover Design by Cali MacKay – Covers by Cali

Edited by Faith Williams – Atwater Group

Contents

THE BILLIONAIRE'S ANGEL

The Billionaire's Obsession Christmas Story

BY

J.S. SCOTT

Prologue

Boston, Massachusetts ~ December 22, 2000

GRADY SINCLAIR PUSHED a stray lock of hair from his eyes impatiently, straightened his glasses with a frown, and then resumed tapping at lightning speed over the computer keyboard in front of him. He was so close, so very close to solving the problem that he'd been wrestling with on this Internet project. He could feel it, and his intuition always made him doggedly driven to solve the puzzle. In fact, being involved in computer projects was about the only place he felt at home, able to forget that he was imperfect, and so much less than his parents wanted him to be.

"I thought I told you to get your stupid ass downstairs and join the party," a furious male voice exploded from the doorway of his bedroom, causing Grady to flinch.

Grady froze at the sound of his father's displeasure, although he really should be used to it by now. When it came to his second-born son, Martin Sinclair was always disapproving, and usually downright hostile. "I'm working on something important," he answered his father quietly and carefully, his stomach dropping to his feet because he already knew what his father was going to say.

The large, gray-haired man folded him arms in front of him, his face red with fury. "Every member of this family attends the Sinclair annual Christmas party. Your sister and brothers are doing their duty, while you're up here hiding away like a coward, an embarrassment to the whole Sinclair name, as usual. My son, the idiot, is not at our party because he's too dimwitted to have a conversation. That's what people are saying." Martin stopped to take a wheezing breath before adding, "You'll show yourself downstairs now and try to act like a Sinclair."

Grady tried not to flinch as he met his father's cold, gray-eyed stare, eyes so very much like his own. "I don't like parties," he stated flatly, knowing it went much deeper than that, but he wasn't about to try to explain. His father had never understood him, and he never would.

"I don't give a shit about what you like and don't like. No son of mine is going to be an idiot *and* a coward. Man up and do what's expected of you," his father growled. "Downstairs. Five minutes. And try not to act like a fool for a change." Martin Sinclair turned around and left without another word.

Grady let out a huge sigh, glad that his father was hosting the annual Christmas party and probably didn't have more time to rake him over the coals for not being the man he wanted *all* of his sons to be.

Martin Sinclair wanted every one of his children to be just like him, and Grady knew he was…different. He didn't want to be, but he was, and at the age of eighteen, he knew he'd never be like his father.

Walking to his closet, he pulled out a suit and tie, shucking his jeans and t-shirt to put on more formal clothing. Nothing less than a suit and tie would do, and if he couldn't act like a Sinclair, at least he would dress like one.

The Sinclair annual Christmas party was something he dreaded every year. And by the age of eighteen, he'd attended a lot of them, every one of them torture. He knew his sister and brothers would rally around him for support. His father would say cutting, degrading things, especially as the evening wore on and Martin Sinclair drank more and more alcohol. His father was a mean drunk, even nastier than when he was sober, which wasn't very often. His mother would be the perfect hostess, just like she always was, never naysaying his father. She never did. She was probably as terrified of his father as her children were, but if she was, she never let on. Her plastic smile would stay affixed to her mouth like it was painted on, a smile that would never quite reach her eyes. Sometimes Grady wondered if his mother was really happy. It was hard to tell.

The Sinclairs were old money, and as high in social status as a family could get. His oldest brother, Evan, was already off to Harvard, home only for Christmas break. Grady envied him, and was counting the days until he could leave for college. Honestly, if he was Evan, he wasn't sure he would have come home for breaks at all. Maybe he could make up reasons why he had to stay on campus when he went to college, avoid the humiliation that always occurred at the Christmas parties. The thing was, Evan didn't feel the same revulsion that Grady did over parties and gatherings. In fact, Grady was pretty sure that Evan was probably downstairs charming every person at the party. His older brother might not be enjoying himself, but he could put on the Sinclair demeanor at will, a trait that Grady admired, but couldn't seem to master. All of his siblings could act the part of a proper Sinclair, a talent that Grady would give his right testicle to have. Hell, maybe he'd give up both of them if he could get relief from his father's constant criticism. Grimacing, Grady cupped his genitals, thinking about losing both of his balls. Okay, maybe not *that*. He *was* an eighteen-year-old guy, and that part of his anatomy seemed pretty critical right now. But he'd give *almost* anything to not be the atypical Sinclair in his family. If he could just fit in, he wouldn't draw anyone's notice.

I'm the odd one out, the disappointing Sinclair.

Grady looked in the full-length mirror, straightening his tie and trying to finger-comb his unruly raven hair into place. He was tall, gangly, and awkward, not yet accustomed to how fast his body had grown in the last two years. He thought about taking off his glasses because then he might not look like such a nerd, and maybe if he couldn't see, it might help block out some of the condescending looks from his father and the guests. But then he'd be stumbling around, unable to see things clearly, which would probably make him look that much more clumsy and stupid. He shook his head, knowing his fear was showing in his eyes, and he hated himself for it. If he could see his own terror in the mirror, he knew everyone else would notice it.

I can do this. I can do this. I do it every year.

Grady stiffened his spine and walked through his bedroom door, the noise of the party assaulting him as he descended the stairs.

His palms grew moist and he swallowed hard, trying to dislodge the lump in his throat as he advanced closer to the crowd, a horde of people who he barely knew. And, as usual, they would be unforgiving, laughing at his bizarre behavior, pitying his father for having a pathetic son. His father only mingled with people who had status and wealth, and for the most part, they were as artificial as his father was, and many were just as cruel.

Why do I have to be different? Why can't I just fit in?

Grady could feel his heart thundering against his chest wall, and he tried to control his rapid breathing, willing himself to take slow, deep breaths.

"Don't let them intimidate you, Grady. You're smarter than every one of them." His brother, Evan, moved up beside him, shoving a plate of food into one of Grady's sweaty hands, and a glass of punch into the other. "Just stay busy eating and ignore them."

Hoping the punch was heavily spiked, he took a large gulp, his eyes meeting Evan's and nodding with a confidence he wasn't really feeling at the moment.

This is why Evan had come home, even when he didn't really want to. He comes because of me.

His brother didn't really want to be here either. Grady could sense it. Evan might try to play the badass young businessman to appease their father, but Evan would never come close to being the man their father was, and he didn't enjoy this crowd. Evan was here for one reason and one reason only: to lend support to his younger brother, Grady.

One by one, his four siblings surrounded him, none of them speaking, but silently lending support.

Grady remained at the fringe of the crowd, his heart pounding, his dizziness never quite subsiding. He promised himself, at that very moment, that this would be the last Christmas he'd ever suffer through this gathering of vultures who had swooped down and humiliated him every single Christmas since he could remember. He would never, ever go through this again!

As it turned out, Grady kept that vow. His father died a few hours later of a massive heart attack, right after the party was over. Martin Sinclair left each one of his children and his wife exceptionally wealthy, and it *was* the very last Sinclair annual Christmas party.

It was also the year that Grady Sinclair admitted he hated Christmas, and always would.

Chapter One

"I CAN'T BELIEVE YOU'RE really going to approach the Amesport Beast for a donation. You're either very brave or very desperate. Grady Sinclair is the last person who would help you out."

Emily Ashworth glanced up from her seat at her office desk, frowning at her best friend and Youth Center volunteer, Randi Tyler. Miranda, better known by everyone in Amesport as Randi, was a local teacher, and volunteered her time at the Center to help kids who needed extra assistance with learning.

"Do I have a choice? He's a billionaire, he lives in Amesport, and we need the money. It's only three weeks until Christmas, and Paul took everything." Emily's eyes drifted down to her computer screen, the balance in the account of the YCOA glaringly showing the numbers in the red. Her ex-boyfriend—if she could even call him *that*—was gone, and so was any money the YCOA had in the business account. Damn it! She should have known Paul was a con, his attention too focused, his pursuit of her too unusual. All his attention and supposed affection was nothing more than a ruse to get his hands on readily available money, funds he shouldn't have been able to steal.

J.S. Scott

It's my fault. I'm the director. I should have watched him closer, not ever left him alone in my office.

Paul had completely duped her, and she'd stupidly fallen for his con job. The bastard! No doubt he had accessed the account from her computer and did the transaction from here. He'd been in to visit her here at the Center two days ago. She'd had an emergency with one of the kids playing basketball and left him alone for a while in her office. The next day, he was gone, and the business account was empty.

"It's not your fault," Randi told her soothingly, plopping her jean-clad butt into the chair in front of the desk. "You had no way of predicting this would happen."

Emily eyed her petite, dark-haired friend warily, wondering if Randi would have been stupid enough to fall for Paul's smooth lines. Probably not! "No matter whose fault it is, I have to fix this. The Center could go under. And we definitely won't have any funds to buy Christmas presents and food this year for the annual party. The gift from us is the only thing some of these kids get every Christmas." Emily's heart sank to her feet, guilt squeezing at her chest. "I can't let the kids down. I can't let the community down."

Amesport was a small coastal town, but the population of kids who needed this youth center was fairly substantial because of all of the surrounding villages. Losing the Center would be a tough blow to the whole town and the surrounding communities.

Randi rolled her eyes. "So you're just going to walk up to Grady Sinclair's door and ask for money?"

"That's the plan, yes. We can get small donations from the community, but we're missing the whole operating budget for the rest of the year. There's no other way to fix this other than to receive a huge donation," Emily replied, sighing as she laid her head down on the desk with her arms underneath it for support, tears of anger and

8

frustration finally escaping from her eyes. "And I don't have the funds to replace it myself."

"I wish I had it to give to you, but I don't have that kind of money lying around either," Randi replied wistfully. "He won't give you the money, so I think you should save yourself the humiliation of asking. Grady Sinclair isn't exactly known for his kindness and generosity. Maybe one of the other Sinclairs—"

"He's the only one in residence. The others are all out of town," Emily replied glumly, already aware that the rest of the family, who all had homes on the Amesport Peninsula, were unavailable. She'd already checked. The last thing she really wanted to do was to approach a man who was known for being rude, antisocial, and condescending. But he was the only Sinclair available. So, beast or not, she was asking. Honestly, she probably deserved to have the guy slam the door in her face. This was entirely her fault, even though the police had already told her that this exact same scenario had occurred in several businesses in Maine in the last few months, but they hadn't yet been able to nail the perpetrator. Still, had she not been so completely charmed by Paul's flattering attention, the future of the YCOA wouldn't be in jeopardy.

Men who look like him don't exactly fall all over me. I should have been suspicious! Paul used his looks and charm to bowl me over, and it had worked because I'm not used to that kind of male attention.

She was tall, her figure too round, and her long blonde hair was usually scraped back into a ponytail. The old pair of glasses perched on her nose didn't help improve her blandness, and she wore very little make-up because most of it irritated her skin. She had a tendency to just blend into the woodwork, and men usually made her a buddy rather than a girlfriend.

"Don't cry over Paul. So what if he was attractive? He's a thief and he's definitely not worth it. I'd castrate the bastard if I could find him," Randi said vehemently. "You obviously weren't his first victim, but I'd certainly like to make sure you were his last."

Lifting her head, Emily swiped at the tears on her face. "I'm not upset about *him*. We only dated for a few weeks, and I obviously didn't even know him. But the kids—"

"The kids will survive, and we'll think of something."

The Youth Center was the heart of the town of Amesport. Not only was the sprawling old brick building a refuge for kids of all ages who needed some support and attention, but it was the place where everything important happened, from wedding receptions to weekly events for the senior citizens in the community. Everything good that took place in town happened here, and Emily would be damned if she'd let the community down by letting the Center go under. The people in this town, from the very young to the elderly, needed this gathering place and the activities and services it offered. She hadn't returned to Amesport only to end up destroying the very Center that she herself had used when she was younger.

Amesport had always been *home* to Emily. The only time she had been away was to attend college in California. She'd stayed there for a while after graduation, trying to climb the corporate ladder, before finally realizing that she really didn't give a damn whether or not she reached the top. When her mom had told her the previous director of the Center had retired, Emily had come back home to stay. It had been comforting that very little had changed during her absence, except for the fact that the Sinclair siblings had all decided to finally claim the peninsula outside of town, land that had been in their family for generations. Grady had been the first to build his home there, with all of the other members of the family putting up their own houses after his was completed. As far as she knew, Grady Sinclair was the only full-time resident on the peninsula, but all five of them had a house there, homes that usually sat empty.

"I have to do something," Emily whispered to herself desperately, standing and pulling on her bright red jacket.

"I hear he eats women and small children as a snack," Randi warned her ominously, her lips curving into a small smirk.

Emily smoothed the jacket over her generous hips and retorted, "I think I'd make a decent lunch." Unlike her petite friend, Emily was far from small, and she'd probably make a decent meal, even for a beast.

She had been back in Amesport and running the YCOA for over a year, but hadn't once encountered a single member of the Sinclair family. Apparently, most of the family was either constantly traveling or lived elsewhere, using their house here in Maine as strictly a vacation home. Grady Sinclair was rarely spotted in town, but his few not-so-friendly interactions with the locals had labeled him as a complete jerk. Residents here in Amesport weren't accustomed to people being less than polite and friendly; almost anyone in town was more than willing to yack and gossip with a new arrival. Apparently, Grady Sinclair wasn't exactly the amiable type, and Emily wondered why he had ever moved here to Amesport. The Sinclairs were from Boston. Sure, they had land here. But then, they owned real estate just about everywhere.

Randi stood, her smirk replaced by a look of concern as she asked, "Are you sure you want to do this?"

"I'm doing it," Emily answered confidently as she scooped up her purse. "How bad can he be?"

Randi shrugged. "I've actually never met him, either. But from what I've heard, he's like the devil incarnate."

Emily rolled her eyes. "Thanks. That's comforting."

Randi grabbed Emily's arm as she made her way to the door and hugged her. "Be careful. Do you want me to go with you?"

Emily was touched that Randi was willing to go confront the beast with her, and she gratefully hugged her friend back. As she released her, she replied, "No. But can you watch over the Center for me? Most of the kids are gone for the evening because there's a storm coming in, but there's a bingo game going on in the recreation hall."

Randi nodded and smiled. "I'll wander over there and lock up when everyone is gone. They usually have good snacks."

Emily gave Randi a mock frown, wishing she had her friend's metabolism and fondness for physical activities. Randi could eat like a horse and never gain an ounce. "Watch yourself. Those ladies get dangerous if you try to swipe too many of their chicken wings," Emily replied with a laugh.

Amused, Randi quipped, "They'll never see me coming or going. I'm an expert at stealing food."

Emily knew Randi meant the comment as a joke, but she knew her friend's background, and didn't doubt there was some real truth in Randi's statement.

"Thanks," Emily told her friend quietly.

Randi gave her a mock salute and a grin as she walked off toward the recreation room.

Emily sighed heavily as she made her way to the exit door, trying not to cringe at the thought of approaching Grady Sinclair. She'd gone up against some intimidating men during her time in California. Sure, he was a billionaire, but he was just a man, right? No different than any other rich guy she'd encountered in her corporate job.

It was dark and snowing as she drove her ancient truck toward the peninsula, knowing it was way past time for new tires, but they weren't really in her budget. Honestly, she bought very little unless it was a necessity. With the cost of paying back student loans, and the low salary she was receiving for her current job, almost everything was beyond her means. She could make more money with her business degree somewhere else, but she'd rather do without than go back into corporate business. She just didn't have the killer instinct to move up the corporate ladder while she was taking someone else down to get there. All she really wanted was to be in a job where she could do something good. And she'd found that at the Center. Unfortunately, she'd made the mistake of dating the wrong guy, which was the story of her life. Granted, the money he'd made off with hadn't been a fortune, but it was a lot to her, money she just didn't have to replace. It was the funds for the expenses of the Center for December, and all the money for the Christmas festivities that had been raised throughout the year. And the sum was way more than she could afford, or hope to get in donations.

"Fat chance the police will have any luck," Emily muttered to herself as she pulled up to the gate that blocked the road to the peninsula. Paul had disappeared as though he had never existed. The police had investigated, but had very little information. Paul probably wasn't even his real name, and he had done this several times before without being caught—if the similar incidents were done by the same man.

Swallowing hard, she stared at the massive metal gate in front of her, wondering how she was going to actually get through it, when the decorative doors started to swing open soundlessly.

It's not locked or guarded. It's motion operated.

Okay. *That* surprised her. In fact, it took her a moment to even give the truck some gas to enter through the open gate. When she finally came out of her perplexed trance, she gunned the engine, making the back end of the truck fishtail on her bald tires. She straightened her vehicle up and kept going. The snow was coming down heavier, a sloppy, wet snow with high winds that signaled an incoming nor'easter.

What did I expect? A guarded fortress?

But yeah, actually, she had assumed there would be some sort of barrier between the ultra-rich Sinclair family and the rest of the world. Even though the peninsula wasn't that large, the Sinclairs owned the entire cape, and the road was private. To be allowed to enter just by driving up to the gate *was* a surprise. When she was a child, the projecting mass of land had sat empty, and she had ignored the No

Trespassing signs more times than she could remember to sit out on one of the shorelines, her very favorite spot on the headland.

My favorite place is in the exact same spot where Grady Sinclair had built his house.

Emily couldn't see well, but she squinted into the swirling snow and pushed her glasses back up onto the bridge of her nose. Passing several private driveways, she kept on going, knowing Grady's home was the very last one.

The road ended at his house, and Emily forged ahead, parking her truck in the circular driveway and turning off the engine.

I must be insane!

Before she had time to think about what she was doing and leave, Emily grabbed her purse and slammed the door of the truck closed. Glad she was dressed in a sweater and jeans for the weather, she just wished she was also wearing a pair of boots, her sneakers slipping and sliding in the fresh, wet snow.

The house was massive, and she gaped at the heavy oak doors in front of her, wanting to run away as fast as her slippery shoes would take her.

"What kind of single guy owns a house this humungous?" she whispered in awe.

Answering herself, she said, "A man who has enough money to donate for the Youth Center."

With that thought in mind, she strode determinedly forward and pressed the doorbell harder than she needed to, causing her feet to slide out from under her and land ungracefully in a heap on Grady Sinclair's doorstep.

That was a fabulous and graceful entrance, Emily. Impress him with your professionalism.

Disgusted with herself, she scrambled for purchase on the icy stone porch, trying to hastily get to her feet before he answered the door, but she slid again and landed flat on her rear end, flinching as her tailbone hit the unyielding surface. "Damn!"

Abruptly, the door swung open, and Emily Sinclair got her first look at the beast from an undignified position on her frozen ass.

Her glasses were wet and foggy, but he looked like no beast she had ever seen. He did, however, look pretty fierce, dark, and dangerous. Without saying a word, Grady Sinclair stuck his hand out as though he completely expected her to take it. She did, grasping his hand as he pulled her to her feet like she was as light as a feather. Trying to straighten up quickly to regain some modicum of dignity, she gawked up at him. She was tall for a woman, but he dwarfed her, towering over her menacingly. He was dressed informally in a tan thermal shirt that stretched across rippling muscles and a massive chest. He was sporting a pair of jeans that looked worn, and he filled them out in a way she'd never seen a man wear a pair of jeans before.

Holy crap! Grady Sinclair was hot. Scorching hot. His dark hair was mussed, and he had a just-rolled-out-of-bed look that made her want to drag him back to a bedroom. Any bedroom. He looked like he hadn't shaved today, and the dark, masculine stubble on his jaw just added to the testosterone waves she swore she could almost feel pulsating from his magnificent body and entering hers, making her squirm just a little at her body's reaction to him.

She drew in a deep breath as his gray-eyed stare seemed to assess her, and finally came to rest on her face. "Hi," she said weakly, unable to form any intelligent words right at the moment. Her brain was mush and her cheeks flushed pink with mortification. This just wasn't the businesslike, graceful entrance she had hoped for, and her lustful reaction to Grady Sinclair had her uncharacteristically flustered.

I need to get it together. I'm acting like an idiot. I need this donation.

He grabbed a fistful of her jacket and tugged her inside, closing the door behind her. Plucking the glasses from her face, he used his shirt to clean them before he handed them back to her. "You don't look like one of Evan's usual women," he said gruffly. "Bedroom is upstairs." He pointed his thumb toward the spiral staircase on the far side of the enormous front room.

Emily stared at him blankly for a moment, and then slanted her gaze toward the living room to try to clear her head. She certainly couldn't seem to think straight when she was looking directly at *him*.

Bedroom? What the hell is he talking about? Evan's women?

"I think you have me mistaken for someone else. I don't know you, and I'm not acquainted with Evan. I came to ask a favor." *Who does he think I am?*

"And you're offering *your* favors for a favor, right?" he asked grimly, his graveled baritone almost disapproving.

Her head jerked back to his face. "What? No. What kind of favor?" she replied suspiciously.

"My brother Evan told me I needed to get laid, which generally is followed by a woman arriving here at my house. I usually just send the women away with a check. But I've decided I'll take you," he said huskily.

Emily gulped. "Someone sends you women…as in prostitutes?" Good God, the last thing Grady Sinclair needed was a hooker. She couldn't think of one single woman who would actually turn him down. "Do I look like a whore?" she asked irritably, suddenly offended by the fact that he'd thought she was for sale. But she felt a shiver of need slide down her spine and land right between her thighs at the thought that he actually wanted her, and what he might do to her if she *was* actually a woman for hire. She wasn't beautiful and she was curvy, her ample figure a little more than most men found attractive.

He reached out and unzipped her jacket, divesting her of the garment and hanging it on a hook by the door. Turning back to her, he said slowly, "Nope. You don't. That's why I want to fuck you."

Emily gasped, his blatant words and heated appraisal making her flush. "Well, I don't know Evan and I don't want to do *that*." *Liar. Liar.* She so *did* want to do *that*, but she wasn't about to admit it when he'd just insulted her. Besides, she didn't do casual sex. "I'm Emily Ashworth and I'm the director of the Youth Center of Amesport. I wanted to talk to you about a possible donation."

She shuddered as his intense, molten gaze swept over her body and back to her face, staring at her with a look so smoldering and hungry that her core clenched in response.

"You're cold," he said abruptly, taking her frozen hand in his and leading her through the living room, down the hallway and into a cheery kitchen. "Sit," he demanded huskily as he dropped her hand, halting at the kitchen table.

Emily sat, so confused that she was unable to make herself do anything else. She watched silently as Grady Sinclair moved around the kitchen, his large body maneuvering with a fluidity of motion that shouldn't be possible for a man as large and muscular as he was. Watching him from behind was almost mesmerizing. She was jealous of the denim that was cupping an ass so tight that she could see the flex of muscle beneath the seat of his jeans as he moved, and it was a view she couldn't bring herself to look away from for some time. Finally, ripping her gaze from him, she let her eyes wander around the kitchen—a bright, airy room with beautiful granite countertops and polished wood floors. Beyond, there was a dining room with a formal, polished wood table, but the room was dim, sparsely furnished, and looked seldom used.

He sauntered to the kitchen table moments later and pushed a mug in front of her, sitting down next to her with his own cup in hand. Emily placed her cold fingers around the mug, sighing as she inhaled the hot, fragrant brew. It was a hot apple cider, and she took a long sip, the warm liquid instantly starting to warm her. "Thank you," she told him quietly as she set her mug back on the table. "So will you consider it?"

"Why?" he questioned darkly, his heated gaze spearing her as she squirmed uncomfortably in her chair.

"The Center needs money."

"Why?" he asked again, lifting a brow as he sipped his drink, his eyes never leaving her.

He knows I'm desperate, that there's a reason I'm here so late asking for money.

"A man I was dating stole the operating money from the Center and we can't keep running without a significant donation," she admitted, wondering why she was feeling the need to be completely honest with him.

Starting hesitantly, she spilled the entire story about the money being stolen as Grady watched her, his expression unreadable as he listened. "So would you be willing to help?" she asked nervously as she finished her story.

He was silent, his expression contemplative as he continued to look at her. Intense minutes passed before he finally answered, "I might be willing to consider it. But I'd want something in return."

She picked up her mug and took another sip of cider, swallowing awkwardly before she spoke again. "What? I'll do whatever I can to get you what you want." The whole future of Amesport depended on his answer. Emily knew she had nowhere else to go and no other solution.

"That's good, because you're the only one who can get it for me," he agreed casually. "Because what I really want is *you*."

Emily nearly choked, sputtering as she swallowed. Dear God, maybe Grady Sinclair *was* the Amesport Beast after all. "I need to give the town of Amesport a Christmas, they need the Center to stay open, and I'll do anything to keep from disappointing the kids there, but I'm not sleeping with you to do it," she told him indignantly.

"We don't need to sleep," Grady replied gruffly. "And I hate Christmas."

How could he hate Christmas? Who hated Christmas except Scrooge?

Emily looked around the massive, tastefully decorated home: not a single red or green decoration in sight. She hadn't seen one Christmas item in his living room, and there was nothing in the dining room or kitchen. "I happen to love Christmas. It's the season of giving and helping others, a time of forgiveness and good cheer."

"Not in my experience," Grady replied, rising from his chair to take his mug to the sink. "It's a time of commercial greed where everyone expects something. Nobody is really happy. It's not real. People are doing what they think is expected of them."

Emily stood up and stalked over to him, rinsed out both mugs in the sink and placed them in the dishwasher. "It's the happiest time of the year." Emily placed her hands on her hips and stared up at Grady, wondering what had made him so cynical. Her irritation drained away as she caught a glimpse of vulnerability in his eyes, a look that told her he wasn't being cruel. He was telling her what Christmas had been like for *him*, and for just a moment, Emily had the craziest compulsion to wrap her arms around him and show him that not everyone in the world wanted something from him.

But even I want something from him. I want funds for the Center.

Grady Sinclair was incredibly wealthy, but there was more to life than money, and Emily wondered if anyone had ever noticed that Grady Sinclair needed more than money could buy. Had anyone ever given him anything, something that couldn't be measured in monetary value?

"I can't have sex with you for money, Mr. Sinclair," Emily told him flatly.

"I'll donate a million dollars," he said huskily, his large body moving closer, pinning her between his body and the sink. "And I'm Grady. I don't want you calling me Mr. Sinclair. Too many of us."

"I can't," she whispered quietly, almost regretting her ethics. "And nobody donates a million dollars to the YCOA."

"I would," he rumbled.

His scent surrounded her as his hands landed on the edge of the sink, a fragrance so masculine that it was intoxicating her. Grady smelled like the ocean, pine, and a tantalizing musk that was uniquely *him*.

Their gazes locked and held; time suspended as Emily began drowning in the swirling, molten pools of gray that reminded her of a storm coming off the ocean. He captured her in the same way as a violent storm, her heart racing as she waited for a force of nature that seemed inevitable.

She didn't really believe he'd donate a million bucks to her Center just to sleep with her, but she'd never seen a man look at her like this, like he needed to have her or die. Unfortunately, Emily had a feeling that she was gazing at him exactly the same way.

"The boyfriend who stole from you…did you love him?" Grady growled, his face a mask of ambivalence, but his eyes were saying something completely different.

"We were only dating for a few weeks. And no, I didn't love him. Obviously he was only after money. He wasn't interested in me." It hurt, but Emily knew it was true. She had been a pawn in Paul's game, a non-person who was disposable.

"Did you fuck him?" Grady asked bluntly.

"No. Of course not. I barely knew him," Emily replied, offended.

"Good." A satisfied look replaced his severe expression. "He was an asshole."

Grady had moved so close that she could feel his warm breath on her cheek, his close proximity making her quiver with need.

"Please," she whispered, although she didn't have a clue what she really wanted. All she knew was that she was caught up in some crazy compulsion that she couldn't seem to break away from. She wrapped her arms around his neck, still held in thrall by the scent of him, the feel of his muscular body pressed against hers.

Without another word, Grady lowered his head and took her mouth with his, and she suddenly knew exactly what she had wanted. Emily surrendered to him with a wanton moan, losing herself completely to the beast.

Chapter Two

GRADY HAD KNOWN he wanted the woman in his arms from the moment he'd seen her sitting on her ass on his doorstep, looking up at him with those innocent blue eyes through crooked glasses, and an embarrassed expression. Emily Ashworth had looked like an angel that had crash-landed on his porch, and he'd been disappointed when he remembered that Evan had threatened to send him another hook-up. That had been the last thing he'd wanted…until he saw Emily. His cock had jumped to attention almost immediately, and all he'd wanted to do was seize the woman, throw her over his shoulder, and make her his as quickly as humanly possible.

Mine.

Spearing his hands through her hair, he groaned into her mouth as the tie holding her hair back gave way, spilling the silky strands over his fingers, caressing his hands like a lover. He felt greedy and desperate, his mouth tasting, his tongue trying to claim her. She tasted like ambrosia, and he couldn't get enough. All he wanted to do was devour her whole, but she'd already said no, which made him even more frenzied. There was something about this woman that was seeping into his skin as he held her, melting the ice around his heart, and starting to relieve the restlessness and loneliness that were his constant companions. It was as exhilarating as it was frightening.

I'm happy being alone. I do what I want, when I want. I like it that way.

Grady was lying to himself, and he knew it. Panicked, he lifted his mouth from hers, an effort that was nearly superhuman.

Fuck. Fuck. Fuck. Separating himself from her that abruptly had been painful.

Glancing down at her just-been-thoroughly-ravaged look, Grady fought not to swoop down on her again and lose himself in her heat all over again.

What the fuck is wrong with me?

"Give me a week, and I'll give you a million dollars." The impulsive comment sprang from his mouth without him thinking about it. "No sex, but I want you to stay here at the house. Just show me Christmas." He was no longer interested in a quick screw for money. Not from her, not from Emily. But he was desperate to get her close to him and keep her there.

Grady's heart was thundering, and his breath was coming heavy in and out of his lungs.

Say yes!

He watched as her brows crinkled in a thoughtful expression. "How?" she whispered in a low, *fuck-me* voice that nearly made him come undone.

He shrugged. "I don't know. I haven't really ever celebrated Christmas. Not the way normal people do, anyway. Make me see it the way you do. Do whatever you usually do here with me."

Oh, hell yeah. He wanted this woman near him, for as long as he could keep her here. His enormous house felt different with her here. *He* felt different.

"You'll really donate money to the Center if I spend a week with you?" she asked, as though she were confused by the whole idea.

"You're not involved with someone else, right?" The question came out casually, but Grady's heart clenched at the thought. Granted, the guy she was dating had just hauled ass with all her money, but there *could* be someone else.

"No. There was just the thief, and even he didn't really want me," she replied sadly, her eyes breaking contact with his to land in the center of his chest.

Grady wanted to break every bone in the asshole's body. His arms came up to stroke her back and he pulled her against him, as though he could protect her from the world. How any man could push this woman away was beyond him. "Was he caught?"

"No," she replied despairingly.

"Give me his information. I'll find him."

"The police can't track him. They're sure it was a false identity."

"I will," Grady vowed confidently. He had so many connections that there was nobody he couldn't track down. "In the meantime, I'll give you the money and you give me your word that you'll spend Christmas with me. What about your family?"

"Only child, a late-in-life surprise for my parents," she replied in a muffled voice against his chest. "Mom and Dad are snowbirds now. They spend the winter in Florida. I couldn't go this year."

The sorrow in her voice made Grady determined to make this the best Christmas season she'd ever had. So what if he personally hated the holidays? Emily obviously didn't, and she was alone this year, just like him. "Then spend it here with me."

She pulled her head back and looked at him with an earnest expression as she asked, "Why me? Why this?"

"Because it's what I want," he answered, knowing it was the truth. "And you said you'd give me what I wanted."

"You promise no sex?" she asked hesitantly.

"Only if you beg," he answered arrogantly, although he was starting to wonder if he might end up being the one pleading. Her sweetness tempted him, and he was going to have a very hard time trying not to devour her.

Pulling away from him, he saw her roll her eyes at his bravado, and it brought an involuntary smile to his lips.

"You have a deal. But I'm bringing a tree and all of my Christmas decorations here," she told him in a threatening voice as he followed her toward the door.

Great. He could hardly wait. He avoided red and green decorations like the plague. But if it would bring her back, she could plaster them in every corner of his house, as long as *she* came along with the red bows and mistletoe.

He helped her into her coat and slammed his feet into his heavy boots, grabbing a jacket from the closet and putting it on as he followed her out of the house.

"This is what you're driving?" he said irritably, his eyes roaming over the bald tires on the small truck. "It looks like a goddamn deathtrap."

The ground was covered in a couple inches of snow, wet and slippery moisture that would have her sliding everywhere on the roads.

"I know how to drive in snow," she replied stubbornly as she opened the door of her truck.

"You need a new vehicle," he replied in a surly tone. She couldn't be driving on the road in this piece of shit. Slapping a hand on the window of her truck, he slammed the door closed and dug in his pocket, bringing out a set of keys. "Drive my truck. It's too slick to drive around with those tires. There's no tread left."

"I can still get some mileage out of them," Emily retorted snappishly. "They aren't that bad."

She was defensive, and Grady immediately knew that she probably couldn't afford it. "Don't you get paid?"

"Not much," she admitted with a sigh. "But I like my job."

"Drive my truck or our deal is off," he grumbled, dangling the set of keys in front of her face.

"I can't take your vehicle," she protested adamantly.

He shrugged. "I have several." He pointed to a huge truck on the other side of the circular drive. "Get into the truck, Emily."

She took the keys reluctantly, drawing a breath to argue as her feet started to skid. Grady scooped her up and bodily carried her to his truck. "Open the door," he ordered, not giving her a chance to argue. She pulled the heavy door open and he deposited her in the driver's seat. "Be careful," he demanded after giving her a rundown of where everything was in the vehicle. "There isn't a lot of snow, but it's slippery. Call me when you get home safe."

"I don't have your number," she said, shaking her head.

"Cell phone," he ordered, holding out his hand.

Emily dug in her purse and handed it to him.

He programmed his number in and handed it back. "Now you have it." Digging in the pocket of his jeans, he pulled out a business card from his wallet and handed it to her. "Take this too." He wanted her to have anything with his name on it, anything to remind her of him, and his contact information available everywhere.

"Are you really sure—"

"I'll have the money transferred into the YCOA account tomorrow. Get me the bank account number." He wasn't about to give her time to second-guess her decision. Hell, he'd wire the money right now if he thought it would get her locked into the deal tighter. "You look tired. You need sleep." He could see the worry showing on her face, and tiny black circles under her eyes. He didn't like it. The desire to see her happy was almost a compulsion, and he was damn near ready to do almost anything to see her smile and remove the signs of stress on her beautiful face.

She shook her head, exasperated, and tucked the card into her purse. "Does anyone ever argue with you or refuse you?" she asked curiously.

"I don't usually ask for anything," he answered bluntly, unable to stop himself from swooping down and kissing her. Her lips warmed beneath his, and Grady wanted to drag her back into the house and warm every part of her body until she begged for mercy. But he stepped back and looked away, closing the door of the truck so she wouldn't get too cold, his protective instincts stronger than his own desire.

He watched the taillights disappear down the road, knowing his life had just changed completely, and he wasn't sure what, if anything, he was going to do about it.

Grady trudged slowly back into the house, divesting himself of his boots and jacket in the foyer, and made his way into his home office.

Picking up the phone, he hoped that Simon Hudson was at home. The two of them had met several years ago, and had become friends almost immediately. Simon had very successfully launched a line of computer games that were still a sensation, while Simon's business partner and brother, Sam, had started a branch of the company that specialized in investments and venture capitalism, the same thing that Evan had done to turn his multi-millionaire status into a billionaire title. Grady and Simon had connected because they were so much alike back then, both of them reclusive computer nerds. But since Simon had met and married his wife, Kara, who had recently delivered a new baby, Simon wasn't the same guy anymore. At one time, Simon's only love had been his computer and his focused drive to design the most challenging computer games on the market. And he'd more than achieved that goal. But now, Simon was completely and totally obsessed with his wife and child. Grady had hoped Simon would get over it, the newness of his relationship wearing off after a while, and turn back into the sensible friend he had known before Simon had met Kara. It didn't happen, and although he and Simon still talked, Grady couldn't begin to understand his friend's obsession with a woman.

Picking up the phone in his office, Grady hit the speed dial, think-ing that if anyone could understand an almost immediate obsession with a female, it was Simon Hudson.

Grady ignored Simon's abrupt greeting and blurted out immedi-ately, "There's something seriously wrong with me. I met this woman today and now I don't feel like myself anymore. I felt literally nau-seous when she left. Shit! Maybe I'm getting the flu. What the hell do I do now?" Grady finished with a huff, his air completely gone.

Simon was silent for a moment before Grady finally heard an evil laugh on the other end of the line. Grady plopped into his office chair and propped his feet on the desk, waiting for Simon to stop laughing uproariously.

"Marry her," Simon replied, his voice actually jovial. "Don't turn yourself inside out like I did. Throw her over your shoulder and take her, kicking and screaming if you need to, and find the nearest justice of the peace. Put yourself out of your misery early, buddy."

"I just met the woman," Grady answered irritably.

"Doesn't matter. If she's already making you crazy, you're screwed. Would you be willing to do anything just to see her again?" Simon questioned mildly.

"A million bucks," Grady admitted. "I offered to donate a million dollars to her charity to spend Christmas with her."

Simon whistled. "You got it bad. You hate Christmas."

"I know," Grady answered wretchedly. "But she wouldn't fuck me, so I was desperate."

"Trust me, the fucking just makes it even worse. Then you'll want her all the time, every minute of the day." Simon hesitated before asking, "Is she worth it?"

Grady thought about that for a minute, remembering Emily's vulnerable expression and how happy he had felt just looking at her and feeling her body pressed against him. "I think so. I mean, I just met her, so I guess it's hard to tell. She seems to take away the loneliness and she made me smile. She's," he paused for a moment before finishing, "different. Not like any woman I've ever met. She wanted a donation for her organization, but she didn't seem interested in anything for herself. She refused to fuck me for money. And I was actually happy about that. Why the hell would I be happy? I wanted her horizontal."

"Maybe because you want her to like you?" Simon mused.

"Nobody likes me except you," Grady answered harshly.

"Who says I like you? You can be a real asshole sometimes," Simon answered, amused.

"And you aren't?" Grady shot back automatically, used to sparring with Simon.

"I say if she can put up with your ornery ass, just marry her. It took me thirty-three years to find a woman who could tolerate me," Simon replied happily.

"I'm only thirty-one. And I think your marriage is a little more than that," Grady said, swinging his feet off the desk and swiveling around uncomfortably in his chair. He'd never talked to Simon about Kara much because he'd never understood his friend's obsession with her.

"Yep. She loves me, and I'm a lucky bastard," Simon answered, his tone cocky.

Grady hesitated for a moment before asking reluctantly, "Does it ever go away? You know, the possessive, crazy feeling you get when you first meet a woman who makes you feel that way."

"No," Simon answered seriously. "It doesn't. It gets worse the closer you get to her. But it's worth it if she cares about you in the same way. You'll never feel lonely again, buddy."

Grady contemplated Simon's words for a while, wondering exactly what *that* would feel like. He was close to his sister and brothers, but they all had their own lives, and were rarely together. What would it be like to truly feel like he wasn't alone, to really feel like he was connected to someone who made him feel complete? He'd actually never thought about it before, had never been exactly unhappy with his life, but he'd always known that there was *something* missing. There was a gaping hole somewhere inside him that not even his computers or his siblings could fill, and meeting Emily had somehow made that emptiness seem suddenly pretty damn painful.

"Tell me what it was like with Kara," Grady asked Simon quietly, wanting to hear about what Simon had gone through before he'd finally found happiness. He and Simon were friends, but they usually discussed computers. Grady had reached billionaire status by developing several wildly successful businesses online and then selling them off, and their conversation almost always revolved around work.

Maybe that's because that's all I do.

But his mind wasn't on work, and he wanted to talk about Simon's life, and the wife who had changed his friend so profoundly.

Surprisingly, Simon began to talk, and he didn't stop for over an hour, barely taking a breath, launching into one story after another. Once started, Simon couldn't seem to stop talking about Kara and his new baby girl.

By the time Grady hung up, he wasn't sure if he should be terrified or relieved. Being alone seemed so much easier and so much less complicated than tying himself up in knots over a female like Simon had done.

Then again, I'm not happy like Simon either.

Glancing up at the clock, he realized how much time had passed since Emily had left. Getting up, he looked outside. The nor'easter had definitely arrived in full force. The wind was howling and the snow was whirling around badly enough to be blinding.

She didn't call me.

Visions of Emily hurt or stranded somewhere started racing through his mind, one horrible scenario after the other.

Panicked, he picked up his cell phone and programmed in the number he'd memorized from her phone, putting it back in his pocket, pacing the office like a caged lion, and checking outside about every ten seconds.

She'll call. She probably just got busy.

"Fuck it!" Grady whispered harshly to himself after he'd waited longer than he could handle, pulling the phone from his pocket and punching her number.

He'd managed to wait exactly two minutes from the time he'd hung up with Simon before calling Emily to make sure she was safely home.

Chapter Three

THE MILLION DOLLAR deposit was in the YCOA account the very next morning. In fact, it was deposited shortly after Emily arrived at work. She'd stared at the balance for the Center, dumbfounded and stunned, for almost fifteen minutes before she logged out of the bank account. Grady had actually done it. He'd made a million dollar donation.

The package came in the afternoon, delivered by a teenager who actually worked at the local florist, but had agreed to do an extra delivery for Dr. Pope. The sandy-haired boy had winked at her when he delivered it, telling her cheekily that it was a delivery that had paid very well when she had started digging for money to tip him, which he'd refused.

Turning the package over and over, Emily couldn't figure out *why* she was getting a delivery, but her name was on it, and the delivery boy had been told specifically to deliver it to her personally.

She tore open the large manila envelope and groped inside, pulling out the contents carefully and letting the items fall onto the surface of her desk. There were two cases and she popped open the first one and froze for a moment, staring at a dainty pair of glasses in an adorably feminine frame. She'd actually tried them on in Dr. Pope's office and rejected the choice, reasoning that they were too impractical, but the real reason she'd decided against them had been the cost. They were much fancier and definitely more expensive than something she would have chosen. *What the hell?* Yanking off her regular glasses, she slid the new pair onto her face, the world around her coming into much better focus. Her glasses were old, and they had surface scratches, but she'd lost one of her contact lenses a few months ago and was waiting until she could afford to get more. Snapping open the other case, she wasn't particularly surprised to see that several pair of contacts were in the case, and she was positive they were exactly the right prescription. Dr. Pope knew exactly what she needed. She'd just had her eye exam a few months ago, and was waiting until she could afford what she needed.

Emily squealed loud enough to bring Randi running into her office, the brunette's face panicked. "What happened?" she asked breathlessly.

"I got new glasses. And contacts. I can't believe my mom and dad did this for me. They live on a fixed income. They really can't afford it." Emily's eyes started to tear at the thought of her parents sacrificing for her. She didn't even remember telling them she had lost her old contacts. Usually she avoided bad news. Her parents were getting on in years, and she tried to keep to the happier stuff when she spoke with them because they worried.

Randi came to the desk and sifted through the contents. "Um… Em…I don't think it was from your parents." Randi dangled a card from her fingertips before handing it to Emily.

It was Dr. Pope's card, but on the back, written in script, was Grady Sinclair's name and simply the word "Paid."

"Grady? Why?" she whispered to herself, running her index finger over the card.

Randi raised a brow, asking curiously, "Is there something you haven't told me about your little visit with Grady Sinclair?"

Emily had asked Randi earlier not to ever refer to Grady by anything other than his name. He'd saved her ass, asking for very little in return except her company for Christmas. And why he wanted *that* she still hadn't figured out. "No. We talked. He made me drive his truck because he was worried about my bad tires. And I left." Okay, she was omitting the tiny little detail that Grady had mistaken her for woman who traded sex for money. And she wasn't about to mention the fact that he'd kissed her. Knowing Randi, she'd blow the whole thing out of proportion. It was just...a kiss. It wasn't like Grady Sinclair actually had any real interest in *her*.

"Obviously you made quite an impression," Randi answered in a teasing voice.

"I can't keep these. Why did he do this?" Emily pulled off the new glasses.

"You need them. Keep them." Reaching out stealthily, Randi snatched Emily's old glasses away from her and put them in her pocket. "Just so you know, these are going to go missing unless you absolutely need them for some kind of emergency. And now...you don't need them." Chuckling softly, Randi scampered out of Emily's office.

"Miranda Tyler, bring those back here." Emily put the new glasses back on and followed Randi, only to find that Randi had grabbed her stuff and left like her ass was on fire.

"Damn." Emily plopped back into her chair in the office. Would they even let her return the glasses now that they had been made for her? Probably not. And she'd be hard-pressed to come up with the money to pay them off.

Grady paid. I have to pay him. Why did he do it?

Emily dug through her purse and pulled out Grady's card. He'd called her last night, sounding almost upset that she hadn't already

called him to let him know she'd made it home. Stopping at the gro-
cery store first, she had just been coming through the door when her
cell phone rang. He'd gotten the account number for the Center's
bank account, and then they had talked about everything and nothing for two hours. Grady Sinclair was blunt, gruff, and okay...maybe
he could be a bit abrupt and intimidating, but the problem was...she
actually liked him. His public image was all wrong, and Grady was
a complete fraud. Underneath his rough exterior was a man with a
good heart. Emily was almost certain of that. There was no artificial
charm or smoothness to Grady, and that made him that much hotter.
He was all male, all the time, and everything feminine inside her
reacted to that, reacted to him.

Shaking her head at her own foolishness, she laid his card on the
desk, and brought up her email.

Dear Mr. Sinclair,

*Thank you for your generous donation to the Youth
Center Of Amesport.*

*I am in receipt of the package you sent today. I hope
you will be able to accept payment arrangements for
the contents. Although I was planning to purchase some
products I needed from Dr. Pope, I hadn't planned to
buy all this right now. It's an unexpected expense that
I haven't budgeted to purchase. Can I make monthly
payments to you?*

Regards,
Emily Ashworth

His reply came through about ten minutes later.

Emily,

Your glasses are scratched and you need them. I used to wear glasses when I was younger, and trying to see around scratches is annoying. If you try to pay me, I'll find a way to get my donation back. And there is no Mr. Sinclair at this email address.

G.

Emily knew she should be angry, but she actually burst out laughing at his reply. There was no professional politeness with Grady. He got right to the point. She sent another lightning fast reply.

Mr. Sinclair,

We've already discussed the terms of our agreement, and this was not part of that verbal contract. Are you going to take the installment payments or not?

Regards,
Emily Ashworth

His reply arrived within minutes.

Emily,

No. I'm not. The agreement was never solid and is still negotiable. I specifically remember you saying you would do whatever you could to get me what I wanted—short of fucking me. That's a pretty broad statement. I wanted to give you the glasses and contacts

as a gift. End of discussion. I also want you to call me
Grady, or you'll pay later for ignoring my request.

G.

It took Emily several minutes to compose herself, shocked and amused by his candid response. She couldn't help herself...she answered.

Grady,

How do you plan to make me pay if I call you Mr.
Sinclair?

Emily

His response was immediate this time.

Emily,

Try it and you'll find out.

G.

Oh, Emily was so tempted. Grady was pushing and she wanted to push back. But sparring with him was dangerous to both her physical and mental well-being. He fascinated and unsettled her at the same time.

Her fingers itched to type a reply, but she deleted the emails and closed the page, determined to ignore her attraction to him. She wasn't used to a man doing anything for her, and she wasn't quite comfortable with Grady's gift. It was too thoughtful, too insightful.

Just the fact that he'd noticed such a small thing about her glasses was perplexing. At the age of twenty-eight, she wasn't a virgin. There had been one boyfriend in college and one after she graduated, but neither of them was anything like Grady Sinclair.

Emily sighed, drew the glasses off her face and inserted the contact lenses. It was a relief to have clear vision again, and the prescription was perfect. Not that she expected anything less from Grady.

Placing the glasses carefully in her purse, she tried to get back to paperwork, but her mind wandered the rest of the afternoon, day-dreaming about what Grady might do to punish her. Chances are, she'd probably love it.

"I want my truck back," Emily told Grady irritably, stomping her foot in what looked to Grady like a female temper tantrum, but he wasn't entirely sure. Most women he knew just took, and they didn't argue.

Emily had just arrived, toting her suitcase and boxes of red and green decorations along with her. She was wearing a Christmas sweat-shirt that shouldn't turn him on, but it did. Decked out in Christmas cheer from her tinkling bell earrings to the Christmas socks he could see quite clearly now that she had taken her sneakers off at the door, Grady decided there was one thing he liked about Christmas now—Emily. Even though she was glaring at him, she looked beautiful decked out for the holidays.

In the last two weeks, Grady had felt like he was losing his mind, his only contact with Emily a brief phone discussion about when she'd arrive at his home, communication that had hardly satisfied his need to be close to her. He'd waited for this day for what seemed like forever, and now she was pissed. But he refused to back down, and honestly, he was finding her temper pretty damn adorable and sexy. "No. I already signed the truck over to you." He was handing her the pink slip to his truck, but she was staring at it like it was a snake that was ready to bite her. "Your truck wasn't safe. You've been driving this one for two weeks. If it isn't what you like, I'll get you something else."

"Of course I like it. It's big; it's completely loaded. God, it even has heated leather seats to keep my ass warm. But that isn't the point. It doesn't belong to me. The only reason I've been driving it is because I don't have my truck. You told me we would trade when I got here for Christmas."

"I lied," he answered, not feeling even a tiny bit of guilt. There was no way he was going to give her back an unsafe vehicle to drive. Her hands were propped on her shapely hips, her eyes staring at the paper he was holding out to her, but making absolutely no movement to take it. "Take it. It's one of the things I want," he said, waving the title in front of her face.

"I want my truck. Where is it?" She ignored the paper being held in front of her, and shot him an obstinate look.

Grady didn't think *now* was probably a good time to tell her that her truck was probably in a scrap metal pile somewhere in another city. "It's gone. It was unsafe to drive."

"It was perfectly safe. It just needed new tires. Give it back."

Grady smirked. "Or what? You'll have me arrested for giving you a better truck?"

"You stole my vehicle," she accused, swatting at the hand holding the title to her new ride.

"I replaced a piece of shit with a brand new truck. It only has a couple hundred miles on it," he told her reasonably.

"Why are you doing this to me?" she asked him, her deep blue eyes confused and vulnerable.

Oh, Christ! Although he liked seeing her all fiery and pissed off, he didn't like her looking *upset*. Those wide blue eyes sucker-punched him in the gut, and he quickly tucked the title of the truck into the back pocket of her jeans and scooped her up into his arms.

He sat on the leather couch, bringing her down on top of him. "What did I do? I thought you'd be happy to have a newer vehicle. Yours sucked," he grumbled quietly, watching her angelic face as she stared back at him and tried to scramble off his lap. "Don't move," he demanded, holding her tighter, but not hard enough to hurt her. Having her shapely rear wriggling against his rock-hard cock was torture, but having her warm, cuddly body pressed against him was worth it. "I'm keeping your ass warm," he informed her in what he hoped was a casual voice. "I thought you liked that."

Emily stopped all movement and her head jerked around to look at Grady. A few seconds later, she burst into uncontrollable laughter, her whole body shaking, her eyes tearing with mirth. "This isn't getting you out of giving my truck back, but I can honestly say I've never had someone offer to be my butt warmer before," she gasped, still trying to recover her breath.

"Your truck is non-retrievable. You'll have to take the newer one," Grady answered, knowing that even if he could get it back, he wouldn't. There was no way his woman was driving around in that old hunk of junk during a Maine winter. "Most people would be happy to have a more reliable vehicle." Honestly, he didn't understand her ire. "Why can't you just take it as a Christmas present? You're the one who said Christmas is all about giving. You're not exactly cheery about getting a gift."

"It's too much, Grady," she answered him seriously, her blue eyes warming as she ran her palm along the stubble on his jawline. "I appreciate it, but I can't take a gift that expensive."

He shrugged. "It's not expensive to me. Shouldn't a gift be relative to what someone can afford? I have other vehicles. I even have another truck. I'll never even miss it." It was the truth. He'd went out and bought another truck right after he'd decided to give her the one she had been driving.

Emily sighed, her eyes searching his face. "We really are from two different worlds. Having that kind of money is unimaginable to me. I have to budget for everything."

"I don't have to budget. I just write a check and I never miss the money. Please take it, Emily. Let me have peace of mind that you're more secure in shitty weather. Please," Grady asked huskily, hoping she'd say yes.

"Do I have a choice?"

"Not really. I think that deathtrap is probably already scrap metal."

Emily sighed, resigned. "Give me some time, okay? I'm not happy that you made that decision without talking to me first."

Grady shrugged. "You would have said no, and I wouldn't have accepted that. It was easier this way." She might as well get used to it. He was going to protect what was his, and as far as he was concerned, she already belonged to him. He knew she definitely had *him,* whether she wanted him or not.

Dropping her hand, she folded both of them together in her lap, and Grady saw tears begin to stream down her beautiful face.

Fuck!

"I don't know how to deal with this," Emily said, dejected.

"What?" Grady asked, confused.

"I don't understand. I don't know why you're doing this. I'm used to solving my own problems, and I'm not used to having anyone who cares whether I drive an old vehicle or if my glasses are scratched. I'm definitely not accustomed to a man who would donate a million bucks just to spend Christmas with me, thereby saving my ass and maybe my job after another man just used me to get quick access to money." Emily drew a deep breath and added, "I can't figure out your motive and it's driving me crazy. I'm just an ordinary woman. I'm not beautiful or the type of woman any man would lose his mind over.

I'm not worth all this, so the things you're doing make absolutely no sense."

Grady had tried to be patient, but as soon as she finished speaking, he completely lost it.

Chapter Four

EMILY WAS ON her back on the couch, Grady pinning her body to the leather, before she even knew what had happened. Startled, she stared at the fierce expression on his face, looming right above hers, with trepidation. He'd switched positions so fast that her mind was still whirling.

"It's only money. And don't ever say you aren't worth it and that you aren't beautiful," he rumbled angrily. "I grew up with money, I've always had it, and now I have more than I'd need in a hundred lifetimes. I don't give a shit about money. It doesn't make people happy. Rich people can be pretty damn miserable. Maybe it would be worth it to me to actually experience a different kind of Christmas for a change. I think you're worth every stupid thing I give you and a hell of a lot more."

She gaped at him, his words touching a place in her heart that made it ache with sadness. Because right at the moment, she realized that this man *wasn't* happy, and probably never had been. The fact that he hated Christmas should have tipped her off, but she'd been too busy wondering why he was doing anything for her to realize that he was actually hurting. Somewhere deep inside, Grady Sinclair had wounds that weren't visible, but were obviously painful. She'd been too caught up in the money to realize that there was so much more to his behavior than money. In fact, she believed him. The money really did mean nothing to him.

"You don't have to give me anything to spend Christmas with me, Grady. I want to be with you," she answered, feeling the truth in her words. "You didn't need to give so much to the Center, and I don't need an expensive truck. I'm alone this year too," she whispered quietly.

"Not anymore," he answered fiercely. "You have me."

Emily sighed and her body relaxed beneath his. She could have protested that they barely knew each other, that they had never had more than a spectacular kiss and a long phone conversation. But, the truth was, she had felt the connection between them from the very moment she'd looked up at him from her undignified position on his front porch. But she was a practical woman, and she was afraid that Grady Sinclair was heartbreak waiting to happen. "Did you really think I was a prostitute? Do you…um…do that a lot?"

"No. But my older brother Evan seems to think not getting laid on a regular basis makes me irritable," he replied, his eyes still boring into her, his expression intense.

"Does it?" she asked curiously, wriggling a little to see if she could escape her prison, or at least get her arms loose.

"Not any more irritable than I usually am. But it doesn't stop him from trying occasionally."

Emily's arms finally broke free from between their bodies, and she wrapped them around his neck, aching to try to relieve some of the turmoil she could see in his smoky eyes. "Where is all your family?"

His eyes grew darker. "None of us particularly like the holidays. My father was a drunk, and the holidays weren't a good time for my family. Evan is conveniently on business in another country where they don't celebrate Christmas, and my other brothers are working, too. My sister is in Aspen with her latest loser boyfriend who none of us can talk her into dumping because all he wants is her money."

"Then I guess you're stuck with me," she told him lightly, stroking the silky strands of hair at the nape of his neck. This man deserved a happier experience, and she was determined to give it to him.

"You're taking the truck," he mumbled stubbornly.

"I'm putting up a Christmas tree," she warned him. "And I'm baking cookies. You have to listen to Christmas music for a whole week."

He grimaced slightly, but answered, "I don't care. As long as you stay, and keep the truck, I'll negotiate." He leaned down and rested his forehead against hers.

Every nerve in Emily's body was vibrating with need, and it was more than just physical. Grady was holding the majority of his weight from her body with his arms, but his muscular body was still plastered against hers from knees to chest, and she could feel the heavy, hard length of his cock pressing against her core. The heat of his body and the scent of his arousal surrounded her, and all she wanted was to melt against him and…

Bong. Bong. Bong. Bong. Bong. Bong.

The huge wall clock struck six o'clock, shaking Emily from her sensual thoughts. "Oh shit…the party!" She'd been so distracted that she'd completely forgotten that they needed to get to the party at the Center. She wriggled in earnest, knowing she was already late.

Grady sat up, looking like he was extremely reluctant to move. "What party?"

Emily hopped off the couch and to her feet. "The Christmas party at the Center is tonight."

"You're not leaving me already?" Grady grumbled, coming to his feet.

"Of course not," she answered excitedly. "You're coming with me."

"I hate parties," he replied with a reluctant expression.

"You won't hate this one," she promised, grabbing his hand and tugging him toward the door. "Most of the town shows up."

"I'm not dressed for a party," he argued.

Emily eyed his jeans and tan cable-knit sweater that looked and felt very much like cashmere. He looked good enough to eat and she'd savor every bite. "It's casual. You look gorgeous."

He shot her a wicked grin that sent incendiary heat directly between her thighs.

Grady Sinclair was an unholy temptation no matter what he was wearing, and she had to tear her gaze away from his to even make it out the door.

❄ ❄ ❄

Grady went to the party, unable to stop himself from following Emily wherever she led. The woman was like a Pied Piper who led him around by his swollen cock. But the moment they arrived at the YCOA, Emily had to circulate and do her job, so he headed straight for the patio, the guests for the party already arriving and filling the recreation area of the Center. Wishing he hadn't left his leather jacket at the door, he paced the small patio area to keep warm, reminding himself that he wasn't a kid anymore.

I can do this. I need to do this. If being near Emily means I have to conquer my fears, then dammit, I will.

Striding determinedly toward the glass patio doors that he'd slipped out of earlier, he stepped inside and stopped abruptly, the music and noise hitting him instantly, and his gut started to roll with apprehension.

He could see Emily on the other side of the room, helping Santa pass out gifts to the crowd of children around a massive tree. Some of the adults were dancing on the wooden floor, swaying to a sappy old Christmas tune coming from a set of speakers near the dancing area. Grady suspected that this enormous space was probably a basketball court or a sports area for the kids when it wasn't being used for a Christmas party. Honestly, he didn't have time to look that closely because he was overcome with dizziness and nausea, the floor tilting, his vision blurred as he broke out in a nervous sweat.

Fuck! Not now. I can't do this right now.

Grady's hand grasped the frame of the door to steady himself, cursing his own weakness.

"Grady? Are you okay? Are you sick?" Emily had come over and was standing right in front of Grady.

"Hate parties," he reminded her, his voice graveled and weak.

Emily cupped both sides of his head and tilted his gaze to her. He stared into her gorgeous blue eyes, his vision clearing as she said sternly, "Look at me. Don't look anywhere else. Focus on me."

Her concerned, compassionate, beautiful face turned the world upright again, and his hungry gaze looked at nothing but her. Suddenly, everything else faded, and there was nothing but Emily.

Walking backward, she took his hands and led him into the room, her eyes never leaving his. Grady didn't even notice where she was taking him until she halted at the edge of dance floor.

"I need you to dance with me, Grady. I need you to touch me. Can you do that?" she asked in a fuck-me-right-now sultry voice.

She needs me.

All Emily had to do was say that she needed him, and he snapped to attention. If she needed, he was going to provide. He wrapped his arms around her with a masculine sigh, his body relaxing as he felt her warm, curvy body mold itself against him, making everything right with the world. Closing his eyes, he inhaled against her temple, the silky strands of her hair caressing his cheek, her warm breath hitting his neck in comforting puffs of air.

"Emily," he mumbled incoherently, every nuance that was uniquely *her* enfolding him as she wrapped her arms around him, stroking his upper back and the nape of his neck. There was no better feeling than holding this woman in his arms. The Christmas music was even louder here, but it didn't matter. He didn't care about the crowd of people he didn't know or what they were thinking. There was only Emily and the way she fit perfectly against his body.

She didn't ask what was wrong; she just held onto him, clung to him, sinking into him like they'd been doing this forever, and Grady savored it. He moved to the rhythm of the music automatically, and Emily followed, the two of them lost in their own little world.

The songs changed, but they still danced, Emily finally tilting her head and whispering to him, "Okay now?"

Grady opened his eyes and looked around him. Some people were looking at him curiously, but mostly all he could see was people genuinely enjoying themselves. The kids were squealing over their presents, showing them off to one another. And the adults were laughing jovially and talking, gathered together in groups around the food tables. Somehow…he was able to see everything as an adult, and it was just…a party. It was a gathering of people who truly seemed to be having a great time in the company of people they actually *liked*. There wasn't a designer gown or tuxedo anywhere in the room, and these were not the same people who had humiliated him in the past.

"Yeah," he answered gruffly. "Yeah, I am okay." How could he not be absolutely fantastic when he was holding the most gorgeous woman in the room, a woman so warm and sweet that he wanted nothing more than to devour her? "Thanks," he added quietly.

She tilted her head back to look at him with a naughty smile. "No need to thank me. I wanted to dance with the most handsome guy in the room."

Grady grinned. "And you think that's me, huh?"

"I know it is." She winked at him and smiled.

His cock was already hard enough to split diamonds just from holding her. Unable to grow any more engorged, it twitched eagerly, making him swallow a groan. There was nothing he wanted more than to bury himself to the hilt inside Emily and never leave her heat. Dropping his hands to her lower back, he nudged her against him. "I want you so badly I can hardly breathe," he admitted, not caring who heard him.

Her expression turned beautifully aroused, her eyes heated as she glanced back at him longingly. "Kiss me," she demanded breathlessly.

"I'm afraid," Grady answered, falling further under her spell.

"Why?"

"I'm not sure I'll ever be able to stop." He craved this woman more than oxygen, and his need for her was nearly staggering.

He felt her body trembling, and he couldn't deny her or himself any longer. He swooped down and captured her tempting lips, wanting to brand her as his, make sure she never escaped.

Mine!

The kiss was a declaration for him, a fierce possession to let her know he had no intention of ever letting her go. All pretense of dancing stopped as he threaded his fingers through her hair with one hand, holding her head hostage for his marauding mouth. Then, he pressed her hips hard against his groin with his other hand, doing a primal dance that had nothing to do with the holidays.

He demanded, and she gave, submitting herself to his possessive embrace, making him completely lose it.

She's mine.

Grady's need was primitive, and all-consuming, his desire fueled by her submission and passionate response. She clung to him like he was her life raft in the middle of the ocean, and he relished it. All he wanted to do was shelter her, protect her from anything and everything that might harm her, make her smile every single day for the rest of his life.

They broke apart, panting and gasping for breath, staring at each other like they wanted nothing more than to tear each other's clothes off to get closer. Grady nearly groaned at the thought of being skin-to-skin with her, losing himself in her softness.

I need her so damn much.

He and Emily were in the shadows, but he could see some people looking on with smiles and he heard some wolf whistles, approvals of the show he and Emily had just put on. But he didn't care. Something feral inside him wanted her drenched in his scent, warning every man in the room that she was his.

"I guess *everyone* doesn't think I'm the Amesport Beast anymore," he said gutturally, still trying to get his ragged breathing under control.

Emily looked at him, stunned. "You knew people called you that?"

"Of course I knew," he answered hoarsely. "I cultivated the image with my charming personality. As long as people left me alone, I didn't care what they called me."

Emily smacked him on the arm. "I've done everything I can to repair your reputation for the last few weeks. The whole town knows you donated the money to improve the programs here and that you're responsible for us having this party. I thought you were being very unfairly maligned. You were my hero."

Grady liked that thought, and he grimaced at the fact that she had used the past tense in her statement. He wanted to always be her hero, but he shrugged. "I'm not exactly...social. I'm an asshole, and all I really had to do was be myself."

Emily sighed and took a breath to respond, but the words never left her lips. Her face suddenly filled with terror as screams began to fill the room and people scrambled. "P-Paul?" Emily stammered, trying to move out of Grady's arms. "What are you doing?"

Grady's gaze shot to a man standing about ten feet to the side of them, a handgun aimed directly at Emily's head. The guy was wavering, his hands shaking as he held his arms straight in front of him, the lethal weapon slightly tilted. A lunatic, cold, and lifeless gaze trained on Emily told Grady several things at a quick glance: the man was drunk or high, desperate and determined to die.

Oh, fuck no! He'd just found Emily, and he wasn't losing her. The bastard could go screw himself. Shifting their positions, he shielded Emily with his body. He could feel her resistance, but she was no match for his brute strength and the adrenaline pumping through his body. The asshole would have to go through him to get to her.

"This your new boyfriend, Emily?" the gunman asked, taking a few steps closer and waving the gun toward Grady. "Grady Sinclair, the billionaire genius. Did you know he's had agents on my ass for two weeks? I've had to hide like a rabbit, in some of the dirtiest holes imaginable. The police never would have found me without you and your boyfriend's help. This place is going to be surrounded in a few minutes and I'm not going to prison. I'd rather die. But I'm taking you and your asshole boyfriend with me," Paul said, his voice high, desperate and slurred.

"Paul, don't do this. You don't need to shoot anyone," Emily cried, panicked. "We can walk out of here right now. I'll go with you as a hostage so you can get away—as long as you don't use the gun."

Grady gritted his teeth, his jaw tight, turning her further into safety while his eyes never left the dull, dead eyes of the criminal beside him. His arm gripped like a steel band around Emily's waist. "Over my dead body," he growled loud enough for her to hear him.

The bastard might take her, but he'd kill her. Grady could tell by the look on the man's face that he was determined to die and would be more than happy to take him, Emily, and anyone else who got in his way, along with him. In fact, that was exactly what he wanted. The guy had obviously snapped, his sanity gone. The gun that was swaying in Paul's hand was a Beretta semi-automatic and Grady shuddered at the number of kids in the building. Luckily, people were pouring out the front door, taking their children out of danger. "Get ready to run like hell and don't look back," Grady ordered Emily in a harsh whisper, mentally wishing everyone would hurry the fuck up and get outside. But not everyone was leaving. There were men in the building who had taken cover, but it was mostly the women and children who were exiting. The men were staying as back-up, but sending their women and kids out of harm's way.

"Close those doors. Nobody else leaves," Paul screamed in a high-pitched voice.

Go. Go. Go. Grady could see the last of the women stream out the door with the kids, the door slamming shut behind them.

And then, there was silence.

The only thing he could hear was his heart thundering in his ears, his rage at the fact that Emily was still in danger barely leashed. Grady's eyes narrowed as Paul stepped closer, now about five feet from his woman. He watched as the gunman's finger started to twitch on the trigger, the wail of sirens making him edgy. Gut instinct was making the call for Grady, and he knew the time was *now*.

"Run!" he demanded urgently, blocking Emily with his entire body as he lunged for Paul.

The gun fired once as Grady took the asshole down, but it discharged as the two of them were falling, and he took solace in the fact that Emily should be long gone. Finally, Grady let go of the rage that had been simmering inside of him, tearing the gun from Paul's hand and sliding it far across the wooden floor for one of the other men to retrieve. He was seeing red, his entire focus on the man who had hurt his woman, and put her in danger again tonight.

"You'll never hurt her again," he growled, slamming Paul's head against the hardwood floor.

Crack!
Crack!
Crack!

The sound of the bastard's skull hitting the floor was so satisfying that Grady never felt the punches Paul was giving back as Grady pummeled him, not wanting to stop until any threat to Emily was gone, the man beneath him dead.

Several uniformed officers came between them, two pulling Grady off the battered gunman, and two more rolling Paul over to cuff him.

"Easy, man. Let us take over," one of the officers told him as they laid Grady on his back. "You've been shot." The police started holding pressure to Grady's side, his expression somber. Raising his head slightly, Grady could see blood. Lots of blood. He wished it had come from the asshole the police were carting away, but he knew it hadn't. It was his, and he was finally coming out of his haze enough to feel the pain from the wound.

"Oh, God," Grady heard Emily cry out as she dropped to her knees beside him, handing a policeman the weapon she had obviously recovered when he had slid it across the floor. "Grady! Talk to me, love."

"I told you to run, woman. Don't you listen? Are you hurt?"

"No. And I wasn't leaving you. I wanted to shoot him, but I was afraid I'd hit you," she replied, her voice tremulous and scared, making Grady wish he could beat the shit out of Paul all over again.

If Grady wasn't so pissed that she hadn't taken herself out of harm's way, he would have been more touched that she'd been so worried about him that she hadn't run away. "Could you try listening when I'm trying to keep you safe? Stubborn woman," he grumbled, flinching as the cop applied a little more pressure to his wound.

Emily took his hand and threaded her fingers through his, stroking his hair back from his forehead as she answered, "What am I going to do with you?" she asked, forlorn.

"Keep me," he answered, his vision starting to blur. "And don't give me any more hassle about the new truck." Okay...he was taking advantage, but he'd use every bit of leverage he could get at the moment.

"You're going to use the edge you have right now to get me to agree?" she asked hesitantly.

"Yep." He was using whatever he could get.

"Okay," she whispered agreeably. "If it will make you happy, I'll do it. Whatever you want right now."

It made him fucking ecstatic, or as joyful as a guy could be who had just gotten shot. He felt her lips on his forehead right before everything started to fade to black, and decided right then and there that being fussed over by Emily wasn't a bad way to go out.

Chapter Five

EMILY DECIDED ALMOST immediately that Grady Sinclair was probably the worst patient to ever enter their small-town hospital. He'd wanted to leave the minute the doctor had sutured the gaping wound in his side. Luckily, the bullet had just grazed his flesh, but it had left a substantial laceration.

She had cried like a blubbering child when the doctor had said Grady would be okay with some suturing, antibiotics, and an overnight stay for observation. It might have been amusing that Grady had actually been trying to comfort her when he was the one in pain if she hadn't been so shaken and relieved.

It had been her fault—Paul was *her* crazy ex-boyfriend—but Grady had risked his own life to save her anyway. Honestly, Emily didn't think he had even given a thought to his own safety. He had only cared about hers, and the fact that he'd been willing to sacrifice his life to protect her completely floored her. No man she'd ever known, except maybe her father, would have protected her without a single thought to their own safety. Now, she was determined to take care of Grady.

Keeping him in the hospital had been a challenge, and she had gotten desperate and threatened to break her promise to spend Christmas with him if he didn't follow the doctor's orders. He grumbled and protested, but he had finally given in. He'd gotten even grouchier when she refused to leave him, telling her to take her ass home and get some sleep. She slept in the recliner beside his bed, not only because she wanted to be with him in case he needed anything, but because she was afraid he'd get up and leave if she didn't keep him in the bed.

Emily breathed a sigh of relief as she got him back home the next afternoon, more than ready to be away from the hospital and the thoughts that kept racing through her mind about what could have happened to Grady.

"You didn't tell me you got a tree," Emily exclaimed as they entered the house, noticing the huge Christmas tree in the corner of the living room for the first time. It was a beauty, full and lush, and at least seven feet tall. She hadn't noticed it when she'd arrived yesterday, probably because she had been too busy arguing with Grady. And then, too preoccupied with letting him kiss her senseless.

"You like it?" he asked cautiously, grimacing as he moved. "You said you wanted one."

"You're hurting. Do you want some pain medicine?" she asked him anxiously.

"No. Do you like the tree?"

"It's beautiful. I'll decorate it later. Right now I just want to get you to bed." She wrapped her arm around his waist, careful not to put pressure on his wound.

"Sweetheart, those are words I've wanted to hear from you since the moment I met you. And I'm not going to bed unless you come with me," he replied obstinately, raising a teasing brow at her as he added, "Seriously? Do you really think you're going to hold me up if I swoon?"

"Yes. I'm stronger than I look," she told him defensively. Okay... maybe she couldn't hold him up, but she could make his trip to the ground less painful.

"Not that I'm complaining, mind you. Feel free to get as close as you want to get," he told her playfully as he moved slowly toward the stairs.

Emily walked him up the staircase, staying close to him because she needed to be there. She followed him to his bedroom, ready to put him into the enormous bed that looked incredibly inviting.

"Bed," she insisted.

"Shower," he said gruffly. "Are you planning to come with me? I could fall and hit my head. Or I might get dizzy."

She had to bite her lip to keep from smiling. She had no doubt Grady was in pain, but he was playing this for all it was worth. "I'll wait outside the door."

"But what if I need you?" he argued with a weak but wicked grin.

"I'll be close," she said sternly, her hands lifting to start unbuttoning his shirt, knowing the motion to do it himself would be painful for him.

"Not close enough," he said hoarsely. "It's going to take me awhile to get the image of that asshole pointing a gun at your head to go away."

Unfastening the last button, she opened his shirt and had to force herself not to gape at the mouthwatering sight of his bare chest and ripped abdomen; his smooth, warm skin stretched over sculpted muscle had her struggling not to salivate.

I need to be clinical. I have to help him. Grady needs me.

She slipped the shirt over his shoulders and let it drop to the floor. "Um...can you handle it from here?" She gulped, looking at the jeans sitting low on his hips, and the fine trail of hair that ran down into the waistband of his jeans. The man had a body that would tempt a saint, and she certainly wasn't that angelic.

"Nope. Movement hurts. You'll have to do it," he said, deadpan.

Her eyes shot to his face. His expression was stoic, but his eyes were pure wicked heat. Her nipples hardened, and fire slithered from her belly and came to rest between her thighs. Even injured, Grady Sinclair was all masculine temptation for her, an alluring mix of demanding male and boyish mischief who had her wondering if she should laugh or be completely mortified.

"Grady," she warned, licking her parched lips as she looked up at him.

"I need your help, Emily. Please."

She couldn't deny him, and to be honest, she couldn't resist the opportunity to touch him. Her hands were trembling as she reached for the button of his jeans, grateful that there was only one button with a zipper. Honestly, she knew this task would hurt him, the movement required to shower probably excruciating. The arm movements required would pull at his sutures, and the last thing she wanted was for him to reinjure himself. He might be challenging her, but she was knee-deep in this task because she couldn't stand to cause him another moment of pain.

Her decision made, she pushed him toward the master bath that she had seen as they entered the bedroom. His face flashed a moment of surprise and great deal of longing as he moved obediently.

Once in the bathroom, she lowered the zipper down on his jeans, unable to keep from noticing that she had to work around a very large and hard appendage as she started pulling them down and off his hips, taking a pair of silky boxers along with the pants. "You're going to let me do all the work. You stand there and let me help you," she demanded as she motioned for him to step out of his pants now that they were down to his knees.

Before she could think about it and change her mind, she whipped her sweatshirt over her head and let it fall to the floor. Her jeans followed, leaving her feeling completely exposed in only a skimpy bra and panties. After seeing his body, she tried not to fidget with discomfort as she felt his gaze on her. She was body conscious, and wasn't particularly fond of parading around almost nude. But right now, her insecurities weren't as important as Grady.

The shower was fancy, and she had to fiddle with the various controls to get the settings correct, but she managed. Holding open the door of the enclosure, she motioned to a naked Grady. "Get in." His wound was already covered in a protective waterproof bandage, but she'd have to be careful.

He didn't move, his eyes roaming over her body, and filled with desire. "God, you're so beautiful it hurts to look at you."

Emily reached up, pulled the clip from her hair, and let the locks fall haphazardly to her shoulders.

She heard Grady groan, and she knew it wasn't from pain. He really did find her nearly irresistible and attractive. Feminine power surged through her body, her insecurities falling away as she looked at his fierce eyes caressing her body like she was the only woman alive. And God, it was intoxicating.

"Get in the shower, Grady," she told him forcefully, knowing she needed a moment to get her thoughts together. "I have to take out my contacts."

It was the break she needed. She dashed down the staircase in her underwear and grabbed her suitcase, bringing it back upstairs with her so she could get her lens case. Her hands shook as she removed her lenses and placed them in the plastic container, taking deep breaths and trying to remind herself that she was taking care of Grady. He needed her right now.

Stepping back into a bathroom that was now foggy with steam, she heard a groan from the shower and yanked the door open. "I told you not to move," she scolded, completely forgetting anything else except her need to keep Grady from hurting himself. She snatched the soapy sponge from his hand and dropped it to the shower floor. Reaching for his masculine-smelling soap, she lathered her hands and started stroking his body with long, languid strokes, starting with his back, massaging the tense muscles as she worked.

Every inch of Grady's body was solid muscle, and as she moved down to his ass, she could feel the incredibly toned glutes that she'd only admired from afar and covered by denim. They were so much hotter and so very real beneath her fingertips, flexing as she smoothed the soap over them.

Get him clean and into bed.

Finishing the back of his body, she washed his hair, pushing his head forward to rinse. "Turn," she asked him quietly.

He turned compliantly, and she started on his front, nearly moaning as she stroked over the sculpted muscles of his chest.

"Strip," Grady said huskily. "I want you naked right now. If I can't fuck you, I at least want to see you."

"I'm washing you. I don't need to finish undressing—"

"Take it all off or I'll do it," he warned dangerously.

Emily knew he'd do it, and he'd hurt himself. Really, did it matter? She was nearly naked anyway.

She set the soap on the ledge and unhooked the front catch of her bra, pulling the soaked garment off her body. Her panties went down her legs easily, her hands still slick with soap. "I'll smell like you," she told him jokingly, feeling suddenly vulnerable before him. Wringing out the lingerie, he hung them over the door and picked the soap up again.

"Good. I want my scent all over you." He reached out and pulled her against his body, stroking his hand over her back and down, his strong fingers cupping her ass and bringing her aching core against his engorged cock. He moved forward and pinned her body between the tile wall of the enclosure and his overwhelmingly masculine form. "I want you underneath me, moaning my name while I bury myself inside you. I want to watch you come," he said harshly, his breath coming hard and fast.

"Don't," Emily cried, the sound half worry and half longing. "You'll hurt yourself." She pushed lightly on his chest, trying to get him to release her.

"Then I suggest you don't move," he answered in a hoarse, tortured whisper. "Because I have to touch you. I need to touch you. The pain of not touching you is killing me."

Emily released a tremulous breath, staying still as he backed up slightly, their eyes meeting and holding. His were filled with a fierce, covetous need that made her entire body quiver and burn like an inferno. Desire clawed at her, some unknown force locking and fusing them together, making her crave him, wanting him to take her in the most carnal ways possible.

His hands moved over her body, while his gaze stayed locked with hers. He cupped her breasts and his thumbs circled and stroked her nipples into hard, sensitive peaks. It was as if the caress of his fingers fired every nerve ending in her body, making her rock her hips, moaning softly as her whole body trembled. She bit her lip, trying to hold back her pleasure, but it wouldn't be contained.

Grady took his time, exploring the valley between her breasts as one of his hands moved lower, his fingers moving in erotic circles on her sensitized flesh.

"I want to be fucking you right now, but I'll settle for this." His hand moved between her thighs, his fingers delving slowly between her wet folds. "I'll watch you come."

Emily's hands slapped against the tile, her knees weakening as Grady explored leisurely, his fingers stroking from her anus to her clit, over and over again. Each time, his finger barely brushed the tiny bundle of nerves, the bud engorged and needy. Her moan escaped her lips completely, and she whimpered, "Please."

His eyes were blazing with liquid heat as he finally moved his thumb over her clit, but the pressure wasn't enough. Emily's eyes fluttered closed, and she thrust her hips forward, begging for relief from the erotic torture. He rotated from breast to breast with his other hand, pinching her nipple hard enough to send a jolt of electric pulsation through her body, followed by a smooth caress.

"Tell me what you want, sweetheart," he demanded, his heated breath caressing her neck, his mouth close to her ear. "Tell me."

"You," she moaned, her chest heaving as Grady finally moved his fingers over her clit with more pressure, more urgency.

His mouth covered hers, stealing her breath as his tongue invaded, taking away any will of her own. She was consumed by Grady, and he was stoking her body to a fevered state that left her helpless to his marauding tongue and his demanding fingers.

Over and over, his fingers rubbed over her clit, every brush taking her higher. His tongue was mimicking what he'd like to do with his cock, thrusting in and out of her mouth like a man possessed.

Finally, Emily couldn't take it anymore. She moved her hand down to cover his, desperate for a rough, vigorous touch that would send her over the edge.

He was panting as his mouth came away from hers. "Open your eyes. Tell me what you want."

"You know what I want," she gasped, entwining her fingers with his and pushing his fingers against her clit harder, faster.

"Open your eyes. I want to watch you come," he rasped. "Tell me that's what you want."

"Make me come. Please," she pleaded, opening her eyes to meet his feral expression.

He looked satisfied with her answer, and finally gave her what she needed so desperately. Grasping her hand with his, he moved their entwined fingers with bold strokes that had her panting and gasping. "Come for me, Angel. Now."

Emily couldn't have held back if she tried. It was as if he knew exactly what would send her over the edge, and she felt her impending climax clawing at her belly as the pulsation began. Letting out a long moan, she tilted her head back, her eyes never breaking contact with Grady's fierce, possessive, and determined stare.

"Oh, God," she choked out as the climax thrummed through her body, her entire being shaken by an orgasm so intense that she had to reach for the handle on the door of the cubicle to keep herself on her feet.

Grady held her, keeping her steady as he kissed her tenderly, as though he were tasting the last drop of her pleasure, absorbing the last of her ecstasy.

Emily floated down slowly, Grady pulling her close and rocking her body against his as she recovered. She shivered, and he turned her so the hot water was at her back, and that small protective gesture just put her under his spell a little deeper.

"Are you okay?" she asked, worried that he'd strained something. She'd tried to be still, but it was still more movement than he should be doing at the moment.

"I just lived a fantasy. I'm better than okay," he answered, amusement in his voice.

It wasn't most men's fantasy to watch a woman orgasm without having one of their own, but this was Grady, and he was the most unselfish man she'd ever known. His actions and his thoughts made her want to cry for some strange reason. Maybe because he was the first man who ever really gave a shit about making her happy? Her hand slid down his sculpted abdomen and curled around his rigid cock. He was rock-hard, and Emily could almost feel the blood throbbing through the shaft.

Grady groaned, and moved his hand down to take her fingers away from him. "I can't take much more, Angel."

"Let me. Please," she begged, needing to make him feel as good as he had made her feel. "But you have to stay very still," she teased. "No hurting yourself."

"Baby, I already hurt, but not from the damn sutures. I want to be deep inside you right now. I want to be buried in you, in your heat, until I burn."

Stepping back, she ran her hand down his chest, savoring the flex of muscle beneath her fingers. "You'll have to settle for this," she told him in a sultry voice as she followed her hand and dropped to her knees on the tile.

"Emily. No," he said in a husky, tortured groan.

Her hand continued to stroke up and down the shaft as her tongue flicked out to lick the velvety head. "No?" she questioned.

"Oh fuck, yeah," he panted harshly.

Smiling, she took him into her mouth, and did one long suck, bringing a strangled groan from Grady as she repeated it again. She moved her tongue down his long length, and then took as much of him as she could manage. Her hands moved, needing to touch his body, finally settling her palms on his ass and gripping it hard as she devoured him.

"Fuck. Fuck. Fuck," he groaned. "That feels so damn good. I won't last."

His hips thrust, and one of his hands came down to thread through her soaking wet hair, guiding her head as she opened her jaw as wide as she could, trying to take as much of his cock as she could manage. Her throat squeezed tight with every entry, massaging the front of his shaft, bringing a strangled groan from Grady with every thrust. Her fingernails dug into his tight ass, pulling him to her with every stroke.

"Sweetheart...Fuck...I can't...I'll come in your mouth," he growled incoherently.

That was exactly what she wanted. She wanted to taste him, and her hunger for him was ferocious. Sucking harder and faster, she felt him shudder before his hot release flooded the back of her throat, flowing warmly into her as he gasped, threw his head back, and released a satisfying groan of ecstasy.

He tasted tangy, slightly salty, and so completely like Grady.

She protested when he hauled her up before she could get to her feet, not wanting him to lift anything. He brushed off her concern and kissed her passionately, and then pulled her against his chest. He rocked her again, just like he'd done when she'd climaxed.

Emily didn't know how long they stayed wrapped together, their bodies humming and their souls singing. All she knew was a feeling of total happiness, and the sense that in Grady's embrace, she was exactly where she needed to be. She thought she had come home to Amesport, but with Grady, Emily felt like she had finally found her real home.

Chapter Six

"DO YOU WANT to tell me what happened to you at the party?" Emily asked quietly in the dark, her body spooned with Grady in his huge bed.

"I got shot," he answered gravely, his baritone vibrating against her ear.

She knew that he was hedging. He knew exactly what she was talking about. "Before that. Your panic attack," she said patiently.

"I don't like parties," he said hesitantly, stroking his hand along her hip absently.

"It's more than that. But if you don't want to share it with me, it's okay," she told him softly.

She might have ended up going to business school for her MBA, but she'd done her undergrad work in psychology. She recognized social anxiety when she saw it.

"It isn't that I don't want to share everything with you. I'm just not really sure how to explain it," he admitted reluctantly, letting out a long, masculine sigh. "When I was young, I stuttered pretty badly."

"Lots of kids do. And you obviously outgrew it." But she knew it probably hadn't been easy. "Kids can be brutal sometimes. They teased you?"

"Yeah. But it wasn't so much the teasing at school. It was at home."

"Your siblings?" she asked, confused.

"My father," Grady said, his voice rough. "I was a Sinclair, and no Sinclair is supposed to have any defect. I could never get my words out, and my father thought I was stupid. He never let a day go by without reminding me that I wasn't the son he wanted. I was supposed to be social, one of the Sinclair elite. I wasn't. I was a computer geek. I didn't really like business. And I had no desire to play the socialite games. None of it was real."

Emily's heart felt like it was in a vise, seeing visions of a young Grady feeling like he never measured up to his father's rigorous standards. "But you're a genius," she argued. "Look at all you've accomplished."

"Didn't matter. I wasn't like him. And he didn't think I was smart. He thought I was defective. Even though I did eventually outgrow my stuttering, he never saw me as anything but an idiot."

Not sure if she wanted to know, she asked hesitantly, "And the party thing?"

"We had the Sinclair annual Christmas party every year, an event that every Sinclair had to attend. My father was an alcoholic, and he got even more verbally abusive when he was drinking. Since he couldn't claim me or accept me as his son, he did his best to humiliate me every year, showing all of his rich friends that he shunned me, making me the family joke. And almost every one of them went along with it, laughed it up with him about me being the Sinclair moron. I guess it's okay to have one of *those*, but he couldn't exactly claim me as part of *his* family. I was nothing to be proud of." Taking a deep breath, he finished, "I was always…different."

"I'm glad you're different. It's better than being a carbon copy of a mean drunk," Emily said fiercely. "No wonder you learned to dread Christmas. Did you celebrate at all as a family?"

"Only the party," Grady admitted. "We were Sinclairs," he said, as though that explained everything. "We decorated because of the party."

"Where are your parents now?" she asked, wondering if she could strangle his father for putting those kinds of fears and insecurities into an innocent boy.

"My father is dead. He passed away right after the Christmas party when I was eighteen. My mother remarried and moved to Europe. We almost never see her. I think we were a part of her life that she wanted to forget. I don't think she was ever happy," Grady mused.

Emily breathed a sigh of relief. She didn't want to commit murder, and if she was in the same room as his alcoholic father, she might have been tempted. "Are you close to your siblings?"

"As close as we can be considering we're never together," he answered quietly.

She had a feeling they had all suffered from being brought up in a home with very little love and an alcoholic father with a short fuse. "How did you ever turn out so special?" she queried softly.

"You mean different?" he asked, confused.

"No…special. Extraordinary. Incredible."

"You think I am? I'm odd," Grady said nonchalantly.

"You are not odd. You're incredible," Emily answered emphatically. "And don't you ever say you aren't. You're the most unique man I've ever known."

"Is that good or bad?" he questioned, sounding slightly amused. "Unique sort of sounds the same as different."

"It's not. And I think you're the best man I've ever known," she answered decisively. "You are special, Grady. You just don't see it. You're brilliant, kind, giving—"

"Ornery, antisocial, irritating, and the Amesport Beast?" he added.

"None of us is perfect, and the only reason people said that is because they didn't know you," Emily answered with a delighted laugh. "I'm afraid you're going to have to live with your good deeds now because you're the local hero."

"I only care about you. I want to be your hero," he answered hopefully.

She turned carefully, trying not to put any pressure on his wound. Wrapping her arms around his neck, she stroked his hair, her heart flip-flopping as she rested her cheek against his rough jaw. Grady was so much more than her hero. He was becoming her everything, but she simply answered, "You are. Believe me...you definitely are. You probably saved my life." She kissed him lightly on the forehead, wishing she could take away the pain of his childhood. She couldn't, but she could try to teach him that his past didn't have to define his future.

"You know the old Chinese proverb...If you save someone's life, you're responsible for it forever," he answered contentedly.

"Don't worry. I won't hold you to that," she commented lightly.

"I want you to hold me to it. Forever," he said sleepily, wrapping his arm around her waist just a little bit tighter.

Emily wasn't quite sure how to respond. Her heart skipped a beat, but she didn't want to read too much into what he said. He was hurt, exhausted, and under the influence of the pain pill he had taken before they'd crawled into bed.

It's better if I don't say anything. Then I won't get hurt.

It was cowardly, and she knew it, but everything was so real and so incredibly intense with Grady. She wanted to be prepared, because the pain of losing the fragile relationship they were forming would probably kill her.

Exhausted, they fell into silence, and finally slept.

* ❄ *

Grady discovered quite a few new things about Emily Ashworth over the next several days. He learned that she loved Christmas carols, and she sang along with them completely out of tune. But her enthusiasm made up for being a little off-key, so he found it pretty adorable. Her Christmas cookies were out of this world, and she couldn't make them fast enough to keep any around for long. She'd tried to hide some, but Grady had managed to ferret them out almost immediately, sneaking into the kitchen when she wasn't looking and wolfing them down like he'd never had Christmas cookies before. He had… years ago…but they hadn't been anywhere near as good as Emily's. He'd also learned she cried over Christmas movies that were her old favorites. She professed to love them, but they made her cry. What she called "happy tears" weren't really something he was familiar with. Why would someone cry when they were happy?

The laceration on his side was healing, but not quickly enough. Grady relived that first night in the shower with Emily over and over in his mind, his need to bury himself inside her and claim her nearly an obsession. He walked around with a constant erection, but Emily refused to let him do anything she considered physical, so he was in a continual state of frustrated lust.

Still, they were the happiest days he could remember. Doing the simplest of things with Emily was special. And the more time she spent in his house and in his life, the more he knew he was never letting her go. He couldn't even think about not having her with him anymore. He thought of her as his own Christmas angel. And she had landed on *his* doorstep.

Mine!

She was his…she just hadn't realized it yet. Hell, she even had him loving Christmas. It was now his favorite holiday, the memories of the past being obliterated by Emily and all the things she did just for the joy of doing them, never expecting anything in return.

Grady lifted his eyes from his computer for a moment to watch Emily, sitting on the floor of his office, sorting out boxes of paperwork. In a pair of worn jeans and bright red sweater, she was absolutely mesmerizing. With Emily, it wasn't one single feature or personality trait that drew him…it was the entire package. There wasn't one single thing about her that didn't have him completely fascinated. Okay… her stubbornness drove him crazy occasionally, but even the annoyed looks she gave him were pretty damn cute. He watched her face as various emotions changed her expressions: irritation, confusion, concentration, and finally elation when she figured something out.

He had to clench his fists on the desk to keep himself from getting out of his chair behind his desk and taking her right there on the floor. He'd had a small taste of her sweetness, but it wasn't enough. And she'd refused to let him get any more than a kiss since that afternoon, her fear of him hurting himself making her back away every time. There was no sweeter sound than the arousing little noises and moans that escaped from her lips when she was climaxing. Watching her had been the most satisfying experience of his life, and he wanted to see her face when he was deep inside her heat, losing himself in her softness while he pounded her into orgasm.

Grady wasn't sure how much longer he could wait. Watching her like this was torture, and work was impossible, although he was trying to get some stuff done on his current project. If she was close, he wanted to watch her. If she wasn't, he wanted to seek her out. He was pretty much screwed either way.

"How can a billionaire possibly be so disorganized?" she said distractedly, sifting through another box of papers, her brows drawn together in disapproval. "And why do you create these awesome businesses just to sell them off?"

Grady smiled, knowing his filing system drove her crazy—basically because he didn't have one. "I like creating them, but I don't like managing them. Once I'm done putting everything together, I'm ready to start another project."

She glanced up at him with a frown. "But every business you've started has gone on to be a huge Internet sensation."

Grady shrugged. "I get paid well for them. I'm not social, and I don't interact with people all that well."

"What are you working on now?" she asked curiously, pulling another pile of papers out of a box and setting them on her lap. She was determined to organize him.

With his history and personality, it probably wouldn't make sense to her at all, but he answered, "A new social media site."

She was silent for a moment as she stared at him, probably trying to figure out if he was really serious. "Why?" she asked hesitantly.

Grady shrugged. "Because I can, I guess. Those who don't socialize develop social media sites for others who do."

She looked at him incredulously, and then burst into laughter, her delighted shrieks echoing in the large room. "Oh Grady, you're brilliant. And your communication is fine. You just never let anyone really know you. Is there anything you can't do?" She was still holding her stomach and gasping for breath from her fits of laughter.

Get you to let me fuck you.

The one thing he wanted, he couldn't seem to accomplish. Aloud, he said, "I obviously can't file."

"I don't think that it's a matter of not being capable—you obviously just don't want to do it," she answered, her skeptical look challenging him.

Busted!

"Paperwork is boring and tedious," he answered defensively.

"So what…you build an online business with your genius, sell it off and just throw the contracts and everything else into a box when you're done?"

Grady fidgeted uncomfortably, 'cause really, she was pretty damn close to the truth. "Of course not," he said irritably. *I also deposit the check, or get the wire transfer into my bank.*

"Grady Sinclair, I can follow your last five years of work from the mess in these boxes," she told him ominously. "But none of it is organized."

"The tax stuff is all in the computer," he argued, beginning to enjoy himself. Obviously, his record keeping offended her MBA, ultra-organized personality.

"Do you even know how much money you have right now?"

Grady smirked. "A lot." He had a financial manager who kept him on top of things, but he honestly didn't know the exact balance of his accounts every single day. That was why he paid the best in the business to do it for him. "I look occasionally and the balances are always going up, so that's good, right?" Okay…he was yanking her chain a bit, but he loved to watch her reactions.

Emily threw her hands in the air in frustration. "But what if it's not invested properly? What if you could be doing better…but you aren't… because you aren't watching things?"

God, he loved watching her stubborn, protective look. Emily was trying to watch out for *him*, and his heart soared. But the worried look on her face got to him. He got up and walked to where she was sitting and picked up the laptop computer next to her. Holding the computer with one hand, he logged in to a website and handed the computer to her. "My portfolio is fine. See for yourself."

She took the computer from him and stretched her legs out, propping it on her thighs.

He walked back to the desk and sat back down in his chair, watching her face as she flipped from one page to the next, her brows wrinkled in concentration. Smiling, he propped his feet on his desk and crossed his hands over his abdomen. Watching Emily had become his favorite activity. "Happy now?" he asked, after watching her analyze everything for several minutes, catching on to the workings of the portfolio tracker site very quickly. "Do you think my financial manager is doing a good job?"

"He's more than good," she said, her voice dripping with admiration. "He's incredible. Who is he?" Her head was still down, her complete focus on the numbers.

"Jason Sutherland," he answered, disgruntled, and not quite sure he liked the reverent expression on her face as he said Jason's name.

"*The* Jason Sutherland?" she asked, her tone reaching the point of awe.

Grady nodded abruptly, now certain he hated Jason.

"My idol," she sighed, setting the computer to the side as she looked up at him. "He's incredible."

"He's not that great," Grady grumbled, knowing he was lying. Jason was one of the most intelligent men he knew, but he wasn't going to admit it when Emily had that dreamy look on her face.

"He doesn't do personal portfolios. I know you're a wealthy man. Um…okay…really wealthy, but he doesn't do portfolios for anyone but himself. He was already incredibly wealthy when I was in business school. I used to study his investment strategies. And he's so young."

"The same age as me," Grady answered, wanting to not talk about Jason anymore. Emily looked too enthralled, and it was irritating him.

"How do you know him?"

"He's my friend. I've known him since childhood," he grumbled. "I suppose you think he's gorgeous, too?" Most women did, and the female adoration Jason got had never bothered Grady before, but it bugged the hell out of him now.

"Nope. I've never met him, of course, but I don't think he looked the least bit attractive in his pictures. But he's incredibly good with investments," she answered, rising to her feet.

"You don't think he's hot?" Grady questioned, his voice full of disbelief.

"No," she answered quietly, her hips swaying as she moved closer to Grady. "He's too pretty, almost too perfect. I much prefer tall, dark beasts who make generous donations to charities and aren't obsessed with their money." She bent over and kissed him softly, lingering just long enough to make Grady nearly insane.

Her scent enveloped him, and her lips tasted like sweet coffee and sin.

She moved back slowly and rested her forehead against his. "I'm onto you, Grady Sinclair. You donate millions to charity. I thought your donation to the Center was incredible, but you do that all the time, don't you? I saw some of the receipts, and I have a feeling there are a lot more I haven't seen yet."

Grady shrugged and swallowed hard before answering. "I don't need the money. They're all good causes."

"I find men who donate millions quietly to charities without wanting people to know how generous they really are incredibly hot," she said in a husky whisper.

Right at that moment, Grady wanted to donate most of his fortune to charity so Emily would find him even hotter. Christ! If he didn't get inside this woman very shortly, he was going to spontaneously combust.

Mine!

"Did you actually think I was hot for your friend? Were you... jealous?" she asked slowly, as though she didn't believe it was possible.

"Yes," he answered immediately. "He might be my friend, but I wanted to tear his head off because I thought you wanted him. Does that scare you?" Honestly, it kind of scared the hell out of him.

I'm losing my fucking mind. I like Jason. He's a good guy. But one mention from Emily that she admired him, and I'm ready to lose it.

"No. I've just never had a guy who wanted me that much," she answered in a tremulous voice.

"I do," he growled, grabbing her around the waist and swinging her onto his lap.

"Careful," she scolded, trying to wriggle off his lap. "You still aren't healed. Let me up."

He wanted to tell her she was healing him, and his gunshot injury was doing fine, too. "Kiss me first," he demanded, spearing a hand through her hair, but waiting for her to kiss him because she wanted to be as close to him as he wanted to be to her.

"I don't want to hurt you," she said nervously.

"Then you damn well better hurry up and kiss me, or I'm going to expire right here in this chair if you don't." Shit, he was desperate, and he needed some connection to her right now. His cock was trying to burst out of his jeans, and he knew she could feel it cuddling up to her ass. "Stay here and let me keep your ass warm," he told her gruffly, putting mild pressure on the back of her head. "Kiss me."

Emily nibbled on her lip, as though she were considering the risks and benefits. "Are you sure you're okay?"

"I'm dying," he rumbled. "Kiss me or kill me."

Emily giggled and boldly lowered her mouth to his with no further prompting.

Chapter Seven

I'M IN LOVE *with Grady Sinclair.*

Emily knew how she felt about Grady with a certainty that was frightening. There was no wondering if it was true, or any indecision about if that love was the real thing. They'd known each other for such a short time, but he'd had her from the moment he'd helped her up from his porch and cleaned off her glasses for her without a second thought. He'd snatched her heart with that one insignificant but thoughtful gesture, and she'd fallen deeper and deeper as every piece of Grady's puzzling personality fell into place.

Really, he wasn't such a great mystery. He was a man who followed his conscience, led his life the way he needed to for his own happiness, and gave to others because he wanted to do it. And he was lonely, not because he wanted to be alone, but because he only knew how to give.

It made Emily want to give *him* everything he needed, but she was afraid. If she gave everything over to Grady and things didn't work out, there would be nothing left, no pieces of herself to put back together. She loved him just that much, and he had the power to either destroy her or make her deliriously happy. Emily knew that with Grady, there was nothing in between. It was all or nothing.

Trying to turn off her own thoughts, she went to the living room and turned on the Christmas tree that she and Grady had decorated together. It was Christmas Eve, and their dinner was warming, everything finished—including the huge turkey Grady had insisted on, telling her he'd eat the leftovers. Neither one of them talked about what would happen after Christmas. It was as though they were both afraid to burst the bubble of happiness that surrounded them right now.

The phone rang, startling Emily with its shrill ringtone. It was Grady's landline, and it hadn't rung once since she'd gotten here.

Walking to the kitchen, she wondered if she should answer. Grady had gone into Portland, telling her he had business to attend to, but that he'd be back by dinner time.

It could be Grady. Maybe he's going to be late. Answer it.

The number was displayed as private, so she answered, fairly certain it was Grady. "Hello," she said cautiously.

"Where is Grady? And who are you?" a haughty female voice asked Emily.

"I'm sorry. He's not here. Can I take a message?" Uncomfortable, Emily shifted from foot to foot, wishing she hadn't picked up the phone.

"Who is this?" the female voice insisted in a nearly hostile voice.

"I'm Emily. I'm here to visit Grady for Christmas," she answered hesitantly, not wanting to piss off any of Grady's friends or business associates. "Can I tell him who called?" she inquired again.

Emily heard a sound of disgust before the woman answered, "I'm Hope Sinclair. Grady's wife. Get the hell out of my house." The line went dead with a loud, decisive *click*.

Her hands shaking, Emily dropped the phone back into the cradle. Her heart hammering so fast she could feel it pulsating through her body, she quickly turned off all the burners on the stove.

I have to go. I have to go.

The need to flee was clawing at her, adrenaline flooding her body.

I never asked him if he had someone. I just assumed he didn't.

There had never been any talk of Grady having a wife, but what did anyone really know about Grady Sinclair? He kept himself isolated, and maybe she traveled a lot. Or they could be separated. But he should have told her.

Pain sliced through her body, almost making her double over in agony. And with the pain came shame. She'd kissed another woman's husband, did intimate things with him.

"Oh, God," she whispered to herself in an anguished rasp.

No. No. No.

Emily couldn't breathe, couldn't think, wanting nothing more than to get out of the house. She needed air, and she needed to clear her whirling thoughts—none of them good, none of them rational.

"Noooo!" she wailed as she yanked the front door open, jammed her feet into her sneakers, and ran.

There was snow on the ground, but she ignored it, needing to distance herself from the pain that was cutting her to shreds. It was cold, but she'd be okay if she just kept running, just kept moving. Maybe she could outrun the agony of Grady's betrayal.

You don't know the truth. Don't jump to conclusions.

Her rational mind said it wasn't possible, but holy hell, her heart ached, and her eyes were streaming tears, the flow trickling down her face.

Why didn't he tell me?

She stopped, breathless and hopeless, at the shore. She made her way down a fishing dock that had been here as long as she could remember. It was weathered, but still sturdy. Standing at the end of the wooden structure, she looked out at the churning ocean. The sound of the crashing waves calmed her down a little, the turmoil matching the emotions that were slamming into her body all at once.

Pain.

Betrayal.

Fear.

Emptiness.

Despair.

Emily would have trusted Grady with her life, never imagining he'd hidden a secret that would destroy her.

The way he looked at me, the way he treated me...was everything all a lie?

She really needed to leave before Grady got back. Part of her wanted to confront him, but she knew she needed time. She was hysterical, irrational. Her thoughts needed to be clear before she spoke with him or she'd lose it.

She had turned to leave, knowing she needed to go home and get herself together, when her foot skidded along the slippery, icy surface of the dock, making her lose her balance completely. One long slide, her slick sneakers propelling her sideways, and she tumbled into the churning waves with a startled, fearful scream.

✳ ❋ ✳

Grady arrived just in time to hear Emily's scream of terror.

Following her footprints in the snow when he'd discovered she wasn't in the house, the trail had led him here to the dock. Her desperate cry had jerked his head to the end of the wooden structure, and before he could wonder what the hell she was doing on the slippery dock, she was falling.

"Fuck!" he rasped desperately, watching his whole life take a tumble into water that he knew couldn't be more than forty degrees.

He shed his jacket and sweatshirt on the run and dove into the water, the frigid temperature taking his breath away, but he ignored the stabbing pain of the impact. His only thought was to reach Emily.

She was bobbing near one of the dock posts, clinging to the wooden structure as the waves pounded at her body.

"What the hell are you doing?" Grady bellowed over the noise of the rushing water. "You have to get out of the water."

Jesus H. Christ, it was cold. He knew neither one of them would survive if they didn't get out of the water.

"My foot's stuck," she screamed. "Get out of the water, Grady."

He could see her struggling, her head going under to try to get free from whatever had her in its grasp.

"Get out of the water, my ass," he growled, diving under the waves and following her legs with his hand, keeping his other arm around the post to keep from being swept away from her by the waves.

The dock was old and weathered and her foot was lodged in a very large split in the wood, held in place by a bolt that was blocking her shoe from escaping. Grasping her foot tightly, he maneuvered it into a position where he could yank her foot free, coming to the surface gasping for air.

He didn't waste his breath trying to talk. He grasped Emily around the waist and propelled her toward shore in front of him. The dock wasn't very long, and the waves helped, tossing them up on shore with very little effort.

Knowing he had to get them warm and dry, he scooped up Emily, wrapped her in his dry coat and sprinted for the house, ignoring the pain of his circulation returning, and his clumsy motion. Jaw clenched with determination, he moved as fast as he could, clutching Emily tightly to his body.

I have to get her warm. She's not even shivering. She's hypothermic.

He didn't stop once he came through the door. He bolted up the stairs, and set Emily in the chair in his room, and frantically started to strip her down.

Her expression was blank, almost as if she were in shock. Grady tore her clothing as he removed it, desperate to get her out of her wet clothes. Once she was naked, he grabbed towels to dry her body and her hair hurriedly, deposited her in his bed and started piling warm blankets on top of her. "You'll be warm in a few minutes, sweetheart. You'll be okay." He knew he was talking as much to himself as he was to her, trying to reassure himself that she was safe.

Her body started to shiver, and her teeth were chattering, which was a good sign. Her body temperature was rising.

"Get warm," she told him as she trembled beneath the blankets. "I'm okay."

She didn't look like she was okay at all, but her eyes looked up at him with a pleading look that he couldn't ignore. He stripped hurriedly, his own body shivering, a reaction that he knew would raise his body temperature, but it was damn uncomfortable.

After using the towels to dry his own body, he slid beneath the pile of blankets. He doubted that he had much body heat, but he pulled Emily to him anyway, wondering if he could give her any warmth that he had left in his body through the sheer power of his will.

Grady clutched her against him, closing his eyes in relief as he felt them shivering together, their bodies warming.

What if I hadn't come home exactly when I did? What if I had made another stop? Would Emily have died out there, unable to get free?

A mammoth shudder went through his body, but it had nothing to do with his body temperature.

"What if I had lost you? What the hell were you doing out there? That dock isn't safe even in the summer." His voice was graveled and anxious.

Her teeth were still chattering slightly as she answered, "You'd still have your wife," she ground through her clenched teeth, struggling to move away from him.

Grady tightened his hold, not letting her escape. "What? Are you delusional? Talk to me." Maybe she was suffering worse than he thought, because she was uttering complete nonsense. But her body was settling down, and she was only shivering lightly now; his had stopped completely.

"Hope Sinclair," she said with a little more strength. "Your wife." She pummeled at his chest, trying to move away from him. "How could you, Grady? How could you kiss me and act like you cared about me when you have a wife tucked away somewhere? Was all of this just some kind of sick game for you? I was in love with you, you bastard!" Emily stopped fighting and burst into tears, her body starting to rock with heartbreaking sobs.

"Stop. Emily. Stop crying." Christ! He couldn't stand to see her this way. It was ripping his heart from his chest. "I don't have a wife. Hope is my sister. Did she call while I was gone?"

"Yes. She said she was your wife," she sniffed, the sobs halting. "Why would she say that if she wasn't?"

Grady snapped, the sight of Emily in tears unraveling him. He rolled Emily beneath him, trapping her so she couldn't go anywhere. "Because she knows Evan sends women who I don't want to hook up with me. She's helped me out before by claiming to be my wife to get rid of a few of them who didn't really want to take no for an answer." He loved his sister and he appreciated that she wanted to protect him from an unpleasant scene, but he wanted to wring her neck for not checking with him first.

"So you aren't...married?" Emily glanced at him for the first time, her expression vulnerable and shaken.

"She's my sister and I love her like a sibling, but I think being married to her is illegal just about everywhere in the world," he growled fiercely. "I'm fucking obsessed with you, or haven't you figured that out yet? I think about you every damn moment that I'm awake, and then I dream about you when I sleep. There is nobody else. And there never will be. I think I knew it the moment I saw you sitting in the snow on my doorstep. You're mine, Angel. I need you more than I need anything else on this earth. Please don't leave me. Ever." His voice was vibrating with emotion, his eyes burning with a fire banked for far too long. Grady didn't care anymore if Emily owned his emotional well-being. He'd already given it over to her, and she could do whatever she wanted with it. He was hers. And she belonged with him. "Nobody will ever love you as much as I do, or take care of you as well as I will. Stay with me, Emily. I need you."

Grady could feel his heart skip a beat as he waited for her answer.

Say yes. Say yes and I'll never want another Christmas gift as long as I live.

Her eyes were bright with tears as she nodded and murmured, "I love you, Grady Sinclair."

Grady took that answer as a yes because he wanted to, and it was the sweetest affirmation he'd ever heard. Right now, it was the only thing he needed to hear. He lowered his head and kissed her.

Chapter Eight

EMILY OPENED TO him the moment his lips met hers, needing him to forgive her for doubting, for accusing him when he was innocent. She put her apology in her kiss, giving herself up totally to Grady. He'd kept her off-balance from the moment they'd met, her usual rational thinking completely out the window. It wasn't possible to intelligently analyze the way she felt about Grady. He completed her, filling a gaping hole in her soul that had always been empty.

Her once-chilled body burst into flames as Grady kissed her like a man possessed, his tongue entwining with hers, retreating, and then entering again with more force, demanding everything from her.

Yes. Yes. Yes.

His big body shuddered above her as she moaned into his embrace, her hands trying to touch him everywhere at once. Muscles rippled under her fingertips as she caressed down his back and grasped his rock-hard ass, trying desperately to urge him closer to her throbbing pussy. Pulling her mouth from his, she begged desperately, "Please, Grady. I need you."

"Not enough," Grady replied harshly. "But you will."

Pinning both hands over her head, he ran his tongue along the sensitive skin at the side of her neck and nipped her earlobe before adding, "It took me thirty-one years to get a Christmas miracle, and you're worth it. So now I want to savor it," he told her in a graveled voice.

Helplessly, she ground her hips up, her pussy flooding as she felt his hard cock so close, but not close enough. "Savor later. Fuck now," she moaned, desperate to have Grady inside her.

"I want to do everything with you all at once. I've dreamed about this, sweetheart. I've dreamed about having you naked in my bed for so long, I'm about to lose my mind." He continued licking his way down her body, releasing her wrists and moving down to her breasts.

Emily gasped when he laved over one of her nipples, the sensitive peaks responding to the feel of his wicked tongue. He pinched just hard enough to cause her body to jolt, the streak of electricity going straight to her pussy. And then he stroked her nipple with his tongue, sending a flood of warmth through her belly and into her core. "Fuck me, Grady. Please." If she didn't get him inside her, she was going to go completely mad. His body was sending off waves of heat, and they were about to consume her.

"Not yet. I need to taste you first," he replied huskily, his breath warm on her quivering belly. "And I promised to fuck you only if you begged."

Dear God, she was ready to grovel, ready to plead with him to have some mercy. There was only so much heat a woman could take, and she was already reaching her breaking point. "Grady...I can't...I don't," she stammered, unable to form a coherent thought as his mouth stroked over her wet folds, not quite getting to where she wanted him to be, but the feel of his wicked tongue made her hips thrust forward, so damn ready for him.

"You will," she heard him rumble, the vibrations pulsating against her pussy.

His fingers stroked down her outer thighs and came back up the sensitive skin on the inside, getting so very close. "Please." All she could feel was Grady, and the carnal things he was doing to her body. He was touching her, tasting her, breathing in her scent, and it was hot as hell. "Stop savoring. Need you now," she gasped, arching her back as she heard a satisfied groan as he dived in and she lost herself completely.

Grady might be a reclusive sort of guy outside of the bedroom, but there was no hesitance as he devoured her. He was completely uninhibited, tasting her with his entire mouth and tongue, feasting on her like he'd never be satiated.

"Oh...God..." Emily let go and a tortured sound escaped her lips as her ass came off the bed, offering herself up to him, needing more of Grady. She gripped the sheets of the bed, her knuckles white from the strength of her grasp.

He took her legs and pushed them up with her knees bent, opening her to him, completely exposing her to his erotic torment. His tongue lashed her throbbing clit, over and over, every pass driving her higher. No mercy. Grady was on a mission, his laser focus directed on making her come. Hard. And his complete domination of her body was making her come undone.

"You taste so sweet," he growled as he lifted his head. "You're almost ready to come for me."

Emily wanted to say she was beyond ready, but Grady was already completely consuming her again. "I can't do this...I can't...," Emily rasped, her heart galloping inside her chest, wondering if she was going to climax or die. Every muscle in her body was tense, and her orgasm was rushing toward her with frightening speed. It was as terrifying as it was intoxicating, her body never reacting this violently in the past.

It's all Grady. His touch makes me insane.

Her hands dove into his hair, grasping his head as he ate her relentlessly, his tongue now moving hot and heavy on her engorged clit. The tiny bud pulsated and her hips rocked with every stroke of his tongue.

Her eyes closed, and she saw flashes of light in the darkness, her whole body sensitized and electric. Her climax slammed into her like a hurricane, and she let out a moan of complete ecstasy as she found her release so hard that she was helpless to do anything else but lay there and come beneath Grady as he sipped at her climax like it was nectar.

"No more. Please. Fuck me." Emily was frantic, unable to wait another minute to feel Grady's cock inside her. She'd just experienced the most incredible orgasm of her entire life. Still, she needed...more. She needed Grady inside her.

Climbing up her body, Grady positioned himself between her thighs. His expression was possessive and animalistic, his eyes stormy and dark. "If I take you now, I'll never let you go," he warned her gutturally. "Not that I will anyway. You were mine since you landed on my doorstep, Angel." He let his cock slide along her folds, drenching himself in her juices. "Just like this, you feel so good. So warm. So incredible." His hips moved, his shaft sliding through her folds again and again.

"I'm no angel. I'm just a woman who's going to go crazy if you don't fuck me right now." Emily ran her hands down his back and latched onto his fine ass, clawing at him, aching to have him claim her. "I'm begging, Grady. I need you."

"Condom," he growled against the side of her neck.

"I've been on birth control for years for my periods. Do you trust me?" she gasped.

"Hell, yes. And I'm damn glad you trust me, because I'm not sure if I could move right now. Nothing has ever felt this good," he said gruffly, and then swooped down to capture her mouth with his.

Emily could taste herself on his lips, and it only made her need him more. Her legs wrapped around his hips, urging him closer.

Grady entered her like his control had snapped, his cock embedding itself inside her to the hilt. He groaned, thrusting his tongue deeply into her mouth as his cock buried itself into her heat. He retreated and entered again, his groan even more tortured. Pulling his mouth from hers, he rasped, "You're so tight."

"It's been awhile," she panted, wrapping her arms around his neck to hold on tight.

"Mine," he growled, his hips thrusting, his cock entering her again and again.

"Yes," she whispered harshly. "Oh, yes, Grady."

He took her body over, possessing her, claiming her with every stroke of his cock, touching places inside her that no one had ever touched before. He filled her completely, his pace increasing, his body demanding more and more. Emily gave him everything she had to give, moaning and throwing her head back as Grady slipped his hands beneath her ass and started to pummel himself into her with a force that took her breath away.

"Too hard. But I can't stop," he rumbled, sounding tortured.

"Don't stop. Take what you want. I'm right here with you." Emily loved his out-of-control dominance, and she didn't want him tame. "More," she pleaded, reveling in the feel of Grady's cock hammering in and out of her, claiming what belonged to him in the most elemental of ways.

"Love you, Emily," he said fiercely as he pumped into her over and over again.

She wanted to tell him she loved him too, but her climax hit her hard, rocking her body with intense spasms that robbed her of speech. She moaned incoherently, her channel clenching hard around Grady's cock.

His mouth covered hers, swallowing her sounds of ecstasy, and releasing his own groan as her climax milked him. His warm release exploded inside her as he kissed her senseless, as though he were trying to continue to claim her even after he already had her.

Releasing her mouth, he rolled, his cock disconnecting, her body splaying over his. They lay there together, both of them panting and out of breath. The moment she was able to speak, she blurted out, "I love you, too. So very much."

He kissed her forehead, her lips, her cheeks, every spot on her face before he answered, "Stay with me, Emily. Every day will be like Christmas for me."

Emily swallowed back tears, hearing the vulnerability so very clear in his voice. "I want to give you Christmas every day. I want to make you happy, Grady."

"You already do," he said in a husky voice. He shifted her body gently to his side, covered her with the comforter and slid out of bed. Emily sighed as she watched his incredible body move across the room and take something out of the pocket of his soaked jeans.

"Damn. I lost my contacts in the water," she said, disgruntled, just now noticing that her vision was blurred.

Flipping on the light on the bedside table, Grady handed her a velvet box that was waterlogged and dirty. "I'll get you more. It doesn't matter. As long as you're safe. You took several years off my life, woman. You have to stop doing that. And I swear I'm going to clean out every store in the area to supply you with plenty of boots," he said gruffly. "Those sneakers are hazardous to my health."

Emily looked down at the box in her hand, her fingers starting to tremble.

"I wasn't really out on business. I needed to pick this up. I had a good friend who told me that I should marry you as soon as possible. I think it's the best advice that Simon ever gave me." He reached over and flipped open the box.

Emily's breath caught; the diamond inside the box was absolutely breathtaking. "Oh, my God."

"Marry me, Angel?" He pulled the ring from its resting place and tossed the box on the floor.

Emily's tears began to flow like a river down her face. Grady didn't give her much time to answer as he lifted her hand and slipped the enormous diamond onto her finger. "Were you going to give me an option?" She hiccupped on a sob, her heart squeezing so tightly in her chest that she was short of breath.

"No," he answered, shooting her a wicked grin. "But a guy is supposed to ask."

Not able to wait a moment longer, Emily threw herself into his arms, hugging him so tightly she was probably choking him. But Grady didn't complain. He pulled her against him, holding her like he'd never let her go.

"It was going to be a yes anyway," she told him softly, laying her head against his shoulder.

"I know Hope can be convincing, but did you really think I had a wife?" Grady tilted her head up to look into her eyes.

"Honestly, I just reacted. I'm sorry. This is all pretty scary. I've never felt like this before, and I guess I just thought it was all too perfect to be real." She sighed, wondering now how she ever believed it as she looked into Grady's eyes, seeing the intensity of his love for her shining from their smoky depths. "I knew I could end up destroyed and hurt."

"No one will ever hurt you again," he answered hoarsely, his voice pulsating with emotion. Wrapping his arms around her, he pulled her into his lap. "If they do, I'll have to kill them."

Emily smiled against his shoulder, knowing Grady would always have protective, dominant instincts, but she wasn't complaining. His love would always surround her, and she would always feel the same protective feelings for him. "I'll shower you with so much love that you'll learn to love Christmas like I do someday," she told him confidently.

"I'm already liking it. It's Christmas Eve, and I'm pretty damn happy," he replied, his voice muffled against her hair.

"What would it take to make you love it?" She squirmed in his lap, feeling the hard, hot protrusion against her ass.

He moved at lightning speed, putting her on her back as he came over her, his eyes mischievous and wicked. Moving between her thighs, he pinned her hands over her head. "You...in my bed...all night long and all day tomorrow. I think I'd be deliriously happy by the end of tomorrow and love Christmas. I might just stroll through Amesport handing out candy canes and wishing everyone as merry of a Christmas as I just had."

Emily laughed merrily. "I think I'd like to see that."

"You know how to accomplish it," he challenged.

"I promised to show you a merrier Christmas," she said thoughtfully.

"Yeah. Yeah, you did." Grady swooped down and kissed her before adding, "But I thought you weren't going to do what we just did."

"No woman could resist a Christmas present like you," Emily told him with a contented sigh.

Grady broke into a sexy smile that melted her heart, and then he kissed her, a Christmas kiss that promised her forever.

They never made it out of bed until the next evening, and they were both so happily exhausted that it was all they could do to eat, and then take themselves straight back to bed, the candy canes completely forgotten.

But it was the merriest Christmas Grady and Emily had ever had.

Epilogue

ONE WEEK LATER, Grady found himself back at the Youth Center, but he wasn't exactly going reluctantly anymore. Grady Sinclair was throwing a party, and he was actually the host. He'd had very little time to arrange it, but he'd pulled off a pretty decent New Year's Eve bash.

The party was in full swing, the band he'd hired filling the hall with music that had most of the folks of Amesport out on the makeshift dance floor.

He smiled as he watched Emily hugging her parents and laughing. God, she made him happy, and he felt every possessive instinct in his body stand at attention when he saw the flash of his ring on her finger, almost unable to believe she was really his.

Her mom and dad had been surprised when Grady's private jet had picked them up at the airport, but they had taken everything in stride. They'd come to meet him and attend the party to make their daughter happy. Really, Grady thought that was pretty extraordinary. Maybe it was normal behavior for loving parents, but normal was something he'd never experienced with his own mother and father.

Honestly, his childhood *had* been fucked up, but Emily made up for all that and more. If he had to do it again just to find his way to her, he'd do it in a heartbeat. He'd moved to Amesport to finally try to find some peace, but he realized that real happiness couldn't be found in a location. His real joy was Emily.

Grady's eyes strayed to the other side of the room, watching his siblings all gathered together, looking like they were actually enjoying the party, maybe because it had brought them all together again. Hope had come from Aspen, minus her loser boyfriend, and his brothers Evan, Dante, and Jared had all arrived together a short time ago. Even Jason had showed up, claiming he had nothing better to do for New Year's Eve. Grady pretty much doubted that, and he saw the way that Jason was watching Hope. He was almost certain it was the same way that he looked at Emily, and he wasn't sure he liked it. Hope was his baby sister, barely twenty-six, and she had known Jason most of her life.

Well, at least she wouldn't be dating a loser this time.

His wayward thoughts were interrupted as Emily came toward him, her hips swaying in a red cocktail dress that he really thought should be illegal. It clung to her curves and exposed more skin than he thought she should be showing, but she looked so incredibly hot that he was hard the instant she smiled at him.

"I still can't believe you arranged all this. God, you look gorgeous in a tuxedo." She wrapped her arms around his neck and planted a soft kiss on his lips. "You're amazing, Mr. Sinclair."

Grady raised a brow at her, knowing a challenge when he was confronted with it. "I thought I told you that I'd make you pay for calling me that. There's a lot of Sinclairs. I want to be special."

"You never told me exactly how that punishment would work." She'd moved closer, talking to him in her *fuck-me* voice, right next to his ear. "I might like it."

Okay…the party had been a great idea, and it had made his woman happy, but he was ready to take her home now. "I'll show you when we get home." Thank God all of his siblings had their own place.

"Hope apologized. Poor thing. She was mortified when she heard what happened. You shouldn't have told her," Emily scolded lightly. "I like her. I like all of your family."

"It seems strange, all of us together again." Grady wrapped his arms around Emily's waist. "I missed them."

"Maybe they can stay for a while," Emily said hopefully.

"Don't get your hopes up," Grady warned her with a frown. "It's a miracle that we're just all in the same place right now."

"One minute to midnight," a happy male voice pronounced loudly, making himself heard over the music.

Grady snagged two glasses of champagne from a nearby table and brought one to Emily. His siblings, Jason, and Emily's parents all gathered around them, and Grady's heart felt as full as it could possibly get. He was here with the woman he loved, all of their family around them. It just didn't get any better than this.

"I can't wait until later," Emily whispered into his ear in sultry voice.

Okay…maybe it *could* get better later, but he was still pretty damned contented.

"Are you tipsy?" he asked Emily with a smile. She'd told him earlier that she got a little wild when she drank, so he'd made damn sure her glass was full all evening.

"Maybe just a tiny bit," she admitted, holding up her index and thumb with a fair amount of space in between.

"Five."

"Four."

"Three."

"Two."

"One."

The entire hall exploded with cheers, the New Year being properly greeted by the people of Amesport.

After Emily had hugged everyone in the family and bussed them all on the cheek, she grabbed his hand and tugged him onto the dance floor. "Dance with me," she insisted, throwing her slightly intoxicated self into his arms without inhibition.

Grady swooped her up into his arms, letting her feet float slowly back down to the floor. "Happy New Year, Angel."

"Happy New Year, love," she answered, her eyes glowing with happiness. "Tell me your New Year's wishes and I'll make them all come true," she told him with conviction.

Grady smiled down at her. "I wish that you would love me forever."

She smacked him playfully on the arm before letting him swing her into a dance to "Auld Lang Syne." "You already have *that*. Think of something else."

"Impossible, Angel. You already made anything I could wish for come true."

Her eyes started to shine with unshed tears. "I love you, Grady."

He pulled her closer and whispered into her ear, "I love you, too. Thank you for giving me back the holidays. What's your New Year's wish?" He wanted desperately to give Emily anything she wished for and more.

"I wish that you would kiss me," she answered simply.

"I'm a billionaire, and that's the only thing you wish for?" He smirked, but his heart was secretly singing.

"It's what I want. You told me you'd try to give me anything I wanted," she told him in a mischievous voice, tossing his own words back at him.

"Anything you want, sweetheart," he answered, his voice amused.

Two seconds later, Grady had Emily bent over his arm, and he made damn sure that he gave her the sweetest, most passionate New Year's kiss she'd ever had.

~The End~

Other Books in The Billionaire's Obsession series:
The Billionaire's Obsession - Simon
Heart Of The Billionaire
The Billionaire's Salvation

A Mermaid Isle

CHRISTMAS

BY

CALI MACKAY

Chapter One

AIDAN GOT READY to hunker down for the nor'easter that was threatening to hit Mermaid Isle. Maine winters could certainly be brutal, but this storm had veered from its original course and now threatened to be one for the record books. It would guarantee the island a picture-perfect, snowy white Christmas, though that did little to ease the demons that tormented him this time of year.

His pantry was well-stocked, he had a cord of wood for his fireplace, and a generator that should kick in if he lost power. He even had a bottle of whiskey should the need arise, though more often than not, he chose to live with the pain rather than dull it.

It usually helped to stay busy, and he'd found that woodworking and making handcrafted furniture was the only thing that brought him some semblance of peace. Not that it would be enough with the holidays approaching.

The wind started to howl and whistle as icy flakes of snow whipped against the large windows. He stoked the fire and added another piece of wood when there was an unexpected knock at his door, sending his shaggy hound into a barking fit. "Whist, pup."

Who the hell was out in this mess? He then thought of his cousin, Lucy, who'd recently moved in down the road with her husband and was nearly five months pregnant. Panic snaked through his chest as he yanked the door open, worried she was somehow in trouble.

The person on his doorstep wasn't his cousin, and it sure as hell wasn't anyone else he recognized either. She looked like Snow White—porcelain skin with rosy cheeks, black as night hair, ice blue eyes, and lush, naturally red lips. Definitely not a local, though what the hell she was doing out in this bad of a storm, he hadn't a clue. And it was really coming down now. "Can I help you?"

"Aidan Nordson?" When he nodded, she gave him a shy smile, squinting against the snow that lashed at her face. "I'm Chloe Madison—Finn's friend."

"The birdseye maple desk with rosewood and mahogany inlay." He seldom made furniture for anyone but friends and family, since he didn't need the money. However, he did occasionally make an exception if it was a favor to a friend. Chloe had been just that. A favor for his younger brother. Though why the hell she'd turned up on his doorstep, he hadn't a clue—and in a goddamn blizzard, no less. There had to be close to eighteen inches on the ground already, and that didn't include the drifts.

"That's right. The desk for my father." Her smile widened and her blue eyes sparkled with relief, though she still looked a little unsure. "I'm sorry…do you mind if we have this conversation inside? It's freezing out here, and I'm sure I must be letting all your heat escape."

"Yeah, of course. Sorry." He stepped aside to let her in, though, truth be told, he wasn't happy about it. He liked his privacy, and didn't usually let any strangers into his home. On the rare occasion that he'd taken orders for his furniture or had business to conduct, he usually dealt with them in the barn behind the house, which he'd converted into his workroom. "Didn't you get my email? There's a huge storm getting ready to hit. I told you not to come."

"I did get it, but not until I was already hours into my drive up from Boston. Since I was nearly here and this is a Christmas gift, I figured I might as well keep going." She quickly glanced out the window and crinkled her nose. "Although...I didn't think the storm was supposed to be that bad."

"The storm veered from the original prediction, which had it going out to sea. I'm surprised you even made it this far without driving into a ditch or the ocean. The bridge..." Fuck. He shook his head and stifled the groan that rumbled in his throat. "It gets too icy in storms like this and they close it down. You need to go. Now. Before you get stuck on the island."

"But...what about the desk? I came all this way. *Please.*" Chloe grabbed his arm with a grip he hadn't expected, her eyes begging and pleading with him. "I can't disappoint my father. This was supposed to be the perfect gift...and a peace offering."

He sighed, knowing he'd regret this. "Go get warmed up by the fire while I make a call. I might be able to get them to hold off on closing the bridge. Not that you'll survive the drive back to Boston."

A deathly cold washed over him as he thought about her getting into an accident. It had his entire body going stiff, and it took all he had to force air into his lungs and keep the shaking at bay.

Just make the phone call. That was all that mattered right now.

He called the police station and got Janice, their dispatcher. Quickly explaining his situation, he cursed under his breath when she told him that they'd already closed the bridge an hour ago. "It's an emergency, Janice...I have a woman here who needs to get off the island. I can send her down there right now...No, it's not life or death...She'll waive any liability...*Please*...Yeah...ok. I know. Thanks anyway. Stay safe."

What he didn't understand was that the bridge had already been closed an hour, and yet she'd only just arrived at his house. "How did you get onto the island? They put the gates down on the bridge an hour ago and the ferry doesn't run in the winter—or in bad weather, for that matter."

She pressed her plump red lips together into a tiny pout. "Sorry—I hadn't eaten since breakfast and my blood sugar was plummeting and making me woozy, so I stopped in town to grab a bite to eat since they were still open at the time."

Perfect. She was driving around in the middle of a blizzard while woozy. And now she was stuck on the island. "I don't know what to tell you...That bridge is closed and there's no other way off the island. Not to mention, this blizzard is a slow mover and it could literally be days before the snow even stops. And that doesn't necessarily mean the roads will even be passable."

Bloody hell. He'd be stuck with her crashing at his place until the storm stopped. *Longer*, since they'd still have to dig out.

The Siren Song Inn.

And then he remembered that they were closed. Since it was the slowest time of the year, they'd shut down for the holidays to give all their employees the opportunity to spend time with their families and friends.

He swore the universe was conspiring against him.

"I'm really sorry about this. I didn't know the storm had changed course." She pulled her jacket snug around her body, as if it'd keep her warm from his frosty reception. "I'll get going. I saw signs for an inn on the other side of the island."

"It's closed until after the New Year." He let out a weary sigh, and then felt guilty when he saw how miserable she looked for getting herself stranded. "You'll have to stay here. The house is big enough to give you privacy, and we've got plenty of food, wood, and a generator if needed."

"I really appreciate this. Finn...well, he mentioned you like your privacy..." The blush on her porcelain skin deepened as she turned away from him and distracted herself with giving his dog a scratch.

Finn wouldn't discuss Aidan's personal life with anyone, though he likely warned Chloe that he could be a little…gruff. His jaw clenched with pent-up annoyance and anger, but he pushed it away. "Her name's Paisley."

"She's cute—and *huge*. And she can't be more than a few months old, right?" Paisley laid down at Chloe's feet and was rewarded with a belly rub.

"She's part wolfhound and part setter, so I'm sure she still has some growing to do." At least he still remembered how to have a conversation. Sort of. "Why don't I show you to your room? Do you have anything you want to grab from your car?"

Giving Paisley a final belly rub, she stood back up, her long black hair falling in waves over her shoulder. "Actually, I was going to head straight to my dad's in New Hampshire for the holidays once I'd picked up the desk, so I packed a bag. I don't suppose…do you know how long I might be stuck here? My father's expecting me for Christmas."

"I hate to disappoint you, but that's not going to happen. Christmas is in just a few days, and as big and slow as this storm is, we'll be lucky if it's even stopped snowing by then." Reminding himself of just how long he'd be stuck with Chloe had his body going tense, especially when she'd be around for Christmas.

It'd been years since the accident, and yet it hadn't gotten any easier. How could it when it involved his fiancée and their unborn child?

His jaw tightened and his body tensed as he forced the pain and the memories back into the darkness. "You should get your bag while you can still get to your car without needing to shovel it out."

"I suppose so. And thanks…for letting me stay." She let out a deep breath, as if she'd been holding it, and then headed out the door.

Aidan cursed himself, the storm, and the universe for screwing with him, while he waited for Chloe to return. All he wanted was to be left alone with his misery, and instead he was trapped in his house with a complete—albeit pretty—stranger. He might be miserable, but that didn't mean he was blind, and with that black hair, those blue eyes, and her blushing porcelain skin, she was striking.

It didn't help that he couldn't even remember the last time he'd been with someone, and it wasn't long before he realized that it had been Hannah.

He pushed thoughts of his dead fiancée out of his head when Chloe walked through the door, stomping the snow off her boots and onto the mat in his entry, while dragging a suitcase behind her.

Not bothering to ask and ignoring her protests, he grabbed her suitcase and headed for the stairs. "This way."

He showed her to her room, and was pleased to see her eyes go wide. Though he may not get many visitors, he took pride in his home, having designed it himself. Being a post and beam home, he'd showcased the massive timbers and beams with cathedral ceilings, and enhanced the rustic feel with stone. He'd even helped build a fair amount of it, and nearly all the rooms had pieces of furniture he'd handcrafted.

"Wow. It's just gorgeous. And the views…" Chloe turned to him with a smile that lit up her eyes, and then touched his arm as she let out a little laugh. "Well, they're really snowy right now. But I'm sure they're normally stunning."

It was a small gesture—her hand on his arm—and yet it sent a jolt of energy through him and sent his heart racing. His body's reaction to her caught him off guard and had him stepping back, away from her touch.

Her smile faltered and fell as he pulled away, and he found himself inexplicably wanting to ease things between them, though why the hell he cared, he hadn't a clue. He gave his head a small shake, as if it would help him regain his senses and then moved towards the door.

"There's food and drink in the kitchen, towels are already in your bath, and there's WiFi—for now, anyway. If you need anything else, let me know." Aidan was halfway out the door when she stopped him.

"Actually, I'd love to take a look at the desk you made for me. If you don't mind, of course. Or we could do it later…" Her eyes were wide and looking far too hopeful, a hint of a smile returning as if it might persuade him to give in to her request.

"I suppose." He let out a weary sigh, and stepped aside to let her pass, wondering how long it'd be before he regretted his decision to let her stay.

Probably not long at all.

Chapter Two

CHLOE FOLLOWED BEHIND Aidan as he led the way, thinking that for such a tall and muscular man, he moved with the supple ease of someone who'd come by their build through hard work rather than pumping iron and hanging out at the gym. He was also damn good-looking, though she figured he might be, given that his brother, Finn, was nothing short of eye candy—and a great guy to boot.

She and Finn had been great friends in college, and though most of her friends assumed there was something going on between them, the truth was he'd been more like a big brother to her. Aidan, however, seemed to be currently lacking Finn's casual ease and good humor.

Unable to resist, she chanced another glance in Aidan's direction. His dark chestnut hair was thick and just a little unruly, and his hazel eyes were intelligent but haunted. Several days growth left him with a heavy enough stubble to mask his strong jawline, and it only added to that rugged mountain man look. Dressed in a soft plaid flannel, worn jeans that hugged one amazingly fine ass, and oiled leather hiking boots, she sure as hell wouldn't tire of looking at him any time soon.

"This way." Paisley followed after them, her nails clicking on the wide plank hardwood floors. Aidan flicked on a light to a long passage, which was a good twenty degrees cooler than the toasty part of the house they'd just been in. It was lined on either side with windows and connected the main house to what appeared to be a barn, though it was damn hard to know for sure when the snow was blowing around.

And if she thought the passage had been cold, that was nothing compared to the barn. Bright lights popped to life, revealing a massive workroom, which was clean and well organized. The barn had been updated with new floors and walls put in, though the massive beams were once again left exposed, giving it the sort of rustic charm she loved.

She took a deep breath and smiled. "I've always loved that smell. There was a sawmill near my college apartment…"

"The wood—the sawdust. There's nothing better, as far as I'm concerned." His lips kicked up into just a hint of a smile, and damn if it didn't take her aback and send her heart racing. She couldn't even imagine what a full-on smile would do to her. "You were out in the Berkshires, right? Went to school with Finn?"

"Yeah, he was in the dorm room across the hall and was also in a handful of my classes." She always thought fondly of that time period in her life. It seemed so carefree at the time, and a welcome escape from all the responsibilities of home.

As the oldest, everything had fallen onto her shoulders after her mother fell ill and later passed away. But she knew that her full scholarship would be her only chance to escape and live her life, and she refused to give up her dream after she'd worked so hard to make it happen. Her two younger siblings were only a few years younger than her and she knew they'd manage without her.

Aidan's eyebrows perked up in surprise. "Were you also an engineering major then?"

"Nah, I was in bio-chem, but a lot of the core science classes over-lapped." She was happy to see that he looked suitably impressed. She'd busted her butt and managed to land herself a good job with a great company, researching new drugs for a variety of illnesses. Best of all, she was able to send money to help her family, though she swore her father was still disappointed that she'd left them to go to school and then moved to Boston instead of moving back home.

She did what she had to do in order to help with their finances, even if it meant setting aside her true love of art. She'd love to just make pottery for a living, having gotten hooked on it when she took it as an elective in college. But that wouldn't pay the bills and she had responsibilities she couldn't shirk off for her own selfish interests.

Even if her father didn't appreciate any of the sacrifices she'd made.

"Actually, I think I remember you coming to visit Finn." He would have been damn hard not to notice, though the man she remembered as Finn's older brother had been far more relaxed and...happy.

"It's possible." He walked over to a draped piece of furniture and pulled off the drop cloth. "Here you are."

She gasped as her breath caught in her chest and tears sprung to her eyes. Without a single thought, she leapt and wrapped her arms around his neck in a hug. He caught her—what choice did he have?—and though she felt him stiffen, she could see a fire spark in his eyes as he held onto her. Suddenly, she was all too aware of him, his mus-cular body, his strong arms, his full lips—and the fact that she'd just invaded the personal space of this very private man.

With her cheeks flaming hot with embarrassment, she let go of him while mumbling her apologies, feeling absolutely mortified. She forced herself to focus on the desk—*not* on the way her body thrummed with arousal and made her nipples go hard against her sweater as she went slick with need. "I can't thank you enough. I swear, I don't think I've ever seen anything more gorgeous. My father's going to love it."

He had to love it. How could he not when it had been handmade special for him? The desktop was made of a honey birdseye maple with a beautiful compass rose inlay made of mahogany and rosewood. The grain of the wood was intriguing, catching the light so it all but shimmered like satin and silk.

She ran a hand over the desk's smooth surface and had a sudden image of Aidan's large hands running over the wood lovingly. And damn if it didn't leave her wondering what those hands would feel like caressing her skin.

"Well, I'm glad you like it." Aidan's eyes drifted from the desk back to her, and she could tell he still seemed unsettled.

Finn had warned her that his brother had become a bit of a loner, but he hadn't said much more than that. At the time, she hadn't found it at all unusual, since she knew plenty of people who liked their privacy. Yet now that she'd met Aidan, she quickly realized that he was far more than just a loner. She didn't know what had happened to him, but it was clear something had broken the man, and he'd retreated from the world to lick his wounds.

Clearly, he wanted to be left to his misery, and she should leave him be. But she could have sworn she saw something in his eyes, felt something between them when he'd held onto her, and she knew she wasn't imagining it. He made her want to ease his pain and comfort him, but he also stirred something in her that was far more primal. Something that hadn't come alive in a very long time—and she was convinced she wasn't the only one who'd felt it.

"Aidan…" She didn't quite know what to say, but didn't want things to get awkward between them. "I'm sorry if I've made a mess of your holidays." When his brows pulled together and his jaw clenched, she cringed and started rambling, trying her best to make things right between them. "I really appreciate you letting me stay here to weather out the storm—and I'm sorry about that hug. It's just that the desk was gorgeous, and I got carried away, and—"

He silenced her with a hard kiss, his tongue bullying its way past her lips as his large hands held her to him. His body pressed against hers and backed her up against his workbench, pinning her in place and making it impossible for her to ignore his hard length, now trapped between them.

When his kiss deepened, it felt like her world was spinning out from under her. Yet he was there, holding her, anchoring her to him, keeping her from slipping away. Her body felt alive, on fire, as desire consumed her, leaving her tight and swollen and aching for him.

And then he was gone, her body reeling in his absence as he pulled away, shook his head, and then left her there in an empty barn.

Chapter Three

WHAT THE HELL was he thinking? He was a goddamned idiot. Never mind that he'd created and run an innovative tech company worth billions. Never mind that his creations had always been leaps ahead of his competitors. Because after the stunt he'd just pulled? He was an idiot—plain and simple.

He shouldn't have kissed her. Should have kept his hands off her. And he was a total dick for kissing her like he did, and then leaving her there without a word. Finn would kick his ass for it—or try at any rate—and he'd deserve it, too.

What he should do is go and apologize to her. But with his hard-on still raging, there was no way he trusted himself around her, and she was *not* a complication he needed—nor one he was ready for.

Before he had the chance to go speak with her, she rushed past him, no doubt heading for the stairs and her room. He stuck his arm out and caught her, holding her in his firm grasp to keep her from escaping. "I'm sorry, Chloe…I shouldn't have kissed you."

Her stiff body slowly softened in his arms as she let out a weary breath, her eyes settling anywhere but him. "No worries. I get it. It was a mistake."

He tipped her chin up so she'd be forced to look at him, and by the gods, when he looked into those blue eyes of hers, when he felt her curves press against his body, he thought it was a mistake he'd happily repeat. "I don't know that it was… "

It didn't have to mean anything beyond satisfying their needs and passing the time while trapped together during a snowstorm. Just a bit of fun. And why not, given that this was the first time in years that he'd even shown any interest in pursuing anyone—even if for nothing more than sex.

It's not that he didn't have the opportunity for a quick and casual hookup if he wanted it, given that the island filled with tourists every summer. Until just now, he hadn't had even the slightest interest—but damn if Chloe didn't change that. And he was damned if he wasn't going to have her.

She slipped out of his arms and shook her head. "Look, I appreciate you letting me stay here, and…damn, that was a mind-blowing kiss. But I know you didn't mean anything by it."

Now that he'd decided he wanted her, not having her wasn't an option. He hadn't made billions by letting things he wanted slip through his fingers. "I want you, Chloe—and I'll be honest, it's been a very long time since I've wanted anyone at all."

"Are you saying you want to sleep with me?" Her eyes went wide, and he half-expected her to slap him.

"Yes." Bloody hell, it was hard to get that word out. But his cursed hard-on was *not* letting up and at this point that was the part of his body driving the conversation. "I'll make it worth your while."

Her eyes narrowed. "I sure as hell hope that *'making it worth my while'* means you'll be good in bed and that you're not actually offering me money to sleep with you."

He shrugged, not exactly sure how he'd meant it, but refusing to play games. In his experience, it was best to just be direct and honest. "I've got money to burn, so it's not an issue if that's what you want.

But the truth is, this is *not* something I do. *Ever.* I'm stepping out of my comfort zone—*for you*. Because you have me interested, and that's not something I've been in a very long time. Take it any way you need to—I don't care as long as it gets you in my bed."

Okay…maybe a little less direct would have been better, if the look on her face was anything to go by. Her cheeks had flushed to a furious red, her blue eyes were narrowed to slits, and those tiny hands of hers looked capable of murder. Yet he was damned if he didn't want to kiss her anger away—or take that heat and make good use of it.

"Look…I don't know what you're normally used to, but if I'm going to sleep with anyone, it won't be because they paid me to. I'm not interested in your money, Aidan, and any interest I had in sleeping with you is now gone." She shook her head and turned to go when he grabbed her hand and pulled her into his arms.

"Is it really? Because I'm not sure I believe you." He nipped at her bottom lip and then caught her mouth in a greedy kiss as his tongue found hers—tasting, taking, his head filling with her scent of snow and cedar. She softened in his arms as her body pressed against his, and his head started to spin with the want of her.

Was he really going to do this? It had been three years since the accident. Three years since he'd last taken anyone to his bed. After a while, his physical needs got consumed by his anger and his hurt, fueling the misery that had him pushing everyone out of his life.

And now? His body was refusing to stay silent and was demanding that his needs be met.

His kisses slowed, but he'd yet to let go of her, the need to keep her in his arms overwhelming. With his head bent to hers, he tried to slow his breathing. "Say yes, Chloe. Because I know you want me just as much as I want you."

He could see her struggling with her decision, even though he knew it was what she wanted. He doubted it'd have been an issue if he'd gone about it differently, if he'd been patient with her. Instead, he'd let his need push her into a corner, so her back was up and she was on the defensive.

She'd yet to answer him, though he could still see her mulling it over. So he did the only sensible thing. He let her go. "Look, you don't need to answer me just this minute, and obviously, you're still welcome to stay here. But it doesn't change the fact that I want you, and I'm stubborn about getting my way when it's something that's important to me."

"I don't even know what to say anymore. It's not that I don't like you, because clearly, I do. But I've never had a guy demand to sleep with me, or offer me money to do so, and frankly, I don't know if I should be flattered or insulted." She shook her head as if to clear it free of the fog that had settled around it.

"It's been *three years*, Chloe. Three fucking lonely and painful years. And I'm not telling you that because I want your pity." He could hear the anger start to seep into his voice and had to force it back before continuing, taking a deep breath to settle himself. "I'm telling you because I need you to know that this is not something I ever do. This isn't just some stupid game. And yeah—you should be flattered, because I sure as hell didn't mean any offense."

"Three years?" Her ice blue eyes held his gaze, taking him in, but he couldn't bear to have her pity him. He turned away, feeling like a fool, when her words stopped him. "I'll do it."

His eyes locked on hers, half wondering if he'd heard her wrong. "You will?"

"Yes—but *not* for money. I don't care how much of it you have. I can manage just fine on my own. Although...I'd like a little more time. I want to get to know you a little first." She ran a hand through her hair so it fell over her shoulders and looked just messy enough to be damn sexy. "And just so we're clear, this isn't something I normally do either."

He let out a little laugh, as the corner of his lips tugged into a hint of a smile. "I can give you a little more time, though I'm not known for my patience. And once I decide I want something, I let little stand in my way."

"Yeah, well, that's all fine and dandy, but I'm not sure we're playing by your rules right now." She crossed her arms in front of her chest and gave him a smug smile that made him want to take her then and there.

He had to admit, she'd been sweet—almost timid—when they'd first met. But now? It seemed the girl had a backbone and didn't take crap from anyone. If he'd thought he could just steamroll her into doing his bidding, it turned out he was wrong.

Not that he wasn't still getting his way.

"My chili is fine without you adding to it." Aidan all but growled at Chloe as she invaded his kitchen and bumped him away from the stove, adding all sorts of things to the pot. They'd spent the last several hours just hanging out in the kitchen and by the fire, getting comfortable in each other's presence, even flirting and stealing the occasional kiss.

"I know it is. But now, it's not just fine—it's damn good." She gave it all a quick stir and then held out the spoon to him so he could have a taste, a smug look already on her face. "Well?"

He wanted to deny her the satisfaction, but as an explosion of flavors danced over his taste buds, all he could think of was getting another spoonful. Once it had more time to simmer, the taste would be amazingly deep and complex. "Ok. You win. It's damn good. Just the right amount of spice, and smoky too. Hadn't expected that."

"That would be the smoked paprika. My secret ingredient. Surprised you had any." When she smiled at him, he felt his mood lighten further, making him want her all the more.

He wasn't used to having people in his space, his home, his life. And though it still felt awkward, it wasn't nearly as painful as he thought it would be. Maybe it was because the sexual tension between him and Chloe was pushing everything else aside.

A pang of guilt hit him, as if he shouldn't ever be allowed to move past that horrible day, and yet he was somehow finding it just a little bit harder to hold onto his pain. He'd have it back once Chloe had gone and he was left alone once more, but for now, it felt good to focus on something else.

Unable to resist her as she stood there stirring the pot, he sidled up to her and slipped an arm around her waist, pulling her to him as he nipped at her neck. She leaned back into him with a needy sigh that had him going rock hard once more. Reaching around her, he lowered the stove to simmer, and then picked her up by the waist and settled her on the island behind them. "I want a taste of what else is on the menu tonight."

"That can wait until…" Her words trailed off as he shifted her legs apart and nestled himself between them, pressing his erection against her warm heat. Fisting his shirt and pulling him to her, she stole a kiss and then another as he grabbed her hips and nipped along her jawline to her ear, loving how her back arched up to meet his body with hers.

"You had said you wanted a little more time, but sweetheart, I don't think I'm capable of waiting a whole lot longer." His words were spoken against her pearly white skin as one hand drifted to cup her breast and the other ran the length of her thigh, her breath coming in stolen gasps. "And by the sweet sounds you're making, I don't think you want to wait much longer either."

Unfortunately, she was wearing far too many clothes for his liking. He bit her nipple through the fabric of her thin sweater before losing patience with it. Pulling it up over her head, he tossed it aside, giving himself a moment to take in her gorgeous breasts, the full mounds peeking over the raspberry red lace of her bra. And then they were pitched into an inky darkness, Chloe's gasp sounding in the quiet.

Pulling her into his arms, he cradled her against him. "It's all right, love...the generator should kick in momentarily."

She nodded. "It just caught me off guard. Silly, I know." Yet she still held onto him as if she were suddenly chilled—and he was glad for it.

When he kissed her this time, he did so with a tenderness that was in such a stark contrast to all their other kisses, it threw him off-kilter and left him shaken.

What the hell was he doing?

This was just sex. Nothing more than fulfilling a primal need. He had no room in his life for tenderness.

Suddenly, getting involved with Chloe in *any* way seemed like a grave mistake. And yet, he couldn't pull away from her, couldn't let her go. The generator kicked in without warning, leaving him unable to hide away his thoughts before she noticed.

He handed her the sweater he'd peeled off her body only moments earlier. "Maybe we should grab dinner."

When he started to pull away, she wrapped her legs around him and grabbed his shirt. "Look...it seems like you've got a lot going on in that head of yours—and it's none of my business. Believe me, we *all* have our issues. But, I like you and...you said it's been three years. I could be wrong, but maybe you need this—and I don't just mean physically."

She loosened her hold on him, giving him the option to go. He pulled away from her and paced a few steps, trying to wrap his head around what he should do. There was no doubt in his mind that he wanted her—but he also wanted to retreat back into his solitude.

Three years...

It'd be three or four days at the most before Chloe was out of his life, and maybe, just maybe, having her distract him during the most difficult time of the year for him might be exactly what he needed to

get through it. Because even after all this time, his heart ached no less with his loss, nor had his anger abated.

He turned back and cupped her cheek in his hand before stealing a small kiss, and then another. "You're right. I do need this, but I think I also need a little time to wrap my head around things. Do you mind?"

She shook her head no, and then slipped her arms around him and settled her head on his chest. "Take all the time you need."

He was acutely aware of how hard his heart was pounding, and knew she could hear every thumping beat. It made him want to pull away and put some distance between them, and yet he found he didn't have the strength nor the desire to let her go. He kissed the top of her head, and forced himself not to think about it. He needed to take the moment for what it was—a brief reprieve from his misery.

"One of us should give the pot a stir." She kissed the hollow in his neck just above the collarbone, her soft lips warm against his skin, stoking his need for her back to life as her kisses started to wander.

"It's fine...simmering..." Suddenly, she was the only thing he could think of and the last thing he wanted to do was wait. He flicked off the stove and scooped her into his arms, tossing her over his shoulder, unable to keep from smiling when she squealed in surprise. "I'm taking you to my bed. Do you have a problem with that?"

"I'm game if you are." She gave his ass a hard smack as he carried her, his backside clearly far too accessible in her current position.

But two could play that game. With her plump ass cheeks right there on his shoulder, he followed through on the temptation and nipped at them, sending her squirming with a yelp. He tightened his hold with a laugh, when it occurred to him that it had been a very long time since he'd last laughed. "Quit your squirming, girl. Or I'll be tempted to bite harder."

Compared to his six foot three, she had to be nearly a foot shorter than him, and her weight insignificant, allowing him to take the steps with ease. His room was just across the hall from the one he'd put her in, though he wondered just how the next few days would play out and whether or not her bed would even get slept in.

Carefully, he tossed her onto his bed. She'd yet to put her sweater back on, and damn if the girl wasn't a sight to behold. He knelt on the bed and couldn't help but smile when she sat up and stroked his hard length through his jeans, a sultry smile on her lips. "Don't suppose you want to get rid of some of these clothes?"

Cupping her face, he tangled his fingers in her hair and bent down to steal a kiss. "You're a forward little thing, aren't you?" And so different from Hannah.

"Is that a problem?" One eyebrow perked up as she pinned him with a stare and stopped stroking him.

He tossed aside his flannel shirt and then added his tee to the pile. "Not at all. If anything, I really like it—clearly. Though I'll warn you now. I like to be in control. Is *that* going to be a problem?" He needed to be, when he had so little control over so many aspects of his life.

"I don't know." With a casual shrug, her small hands slid over his abs before tugging at his belt. As she undid the button on his jeans, his cock jumped in anticipation, desperate for her. "Maybe...maybe not. Not really used to giving up control. I usually have too many things to take care of—and I want to take care of you."

"I've no doubt you will, love. But it might be good for you to let someone else be in charge then." Biting back a moan as she slipped her fingers around his girth and stroked him, he nipped at her bottom lip and ran his hands over her breasts, taking a moment to tease her nipples before unhooking her bra. He pulled away just enough to catch a glimpse of her dark rose nipples, stark against her luminescent skin. "You're stunning. You know that?"

She ran her tongue up his hard length and then licked the tip, making it jump under her touch. "You're pretty stunning yourself."

Slipping her mouth over the head of his cock, she ran her hands down his length as she devoured him, his fingers tangling in her hair. Her tongue teased him as her lips ran along his length and his hips slowly thrust towards her. Yet he wouldn't last if she kept this up. When he pulled free of her, he loved that she let out a little moan in protest. "You already have me riding that edge, love, and that's not how I want this to go down."

He shucked his jeans before running a hand down her leg to yank off her boots, first one and then the other, all the while drinking her in like she was a glass of ice water and he'd just run a marathon in the desert. From there, it was only a moment more before he'd rid her of her jeans and panties, all in one go, so she finally lay there naked before him.

Coherent thought seemed all but impossible with his heart pounding its deafening beat. It had been too long. *Far* too long, but there was no way in hell he was going to rush through this and not savor every moment. Settling himself between her legs, he stole her breath with a long kiss, his tongue dancing over hers as her warm, supple body shifted below him, as if searching him out.

He laughed against her lips. "Patience, love. We'll get to that too."

Pushing away his urgency, he forced himself to take things slow, to take in every detail of her—the quick pulse at her throat, her lush curves, her silky skin. He trailed a lazy line of kisses down her neck to her breasts, pausing to pull the pert buds into his mouth, loving the needy whimpers that escaped her lips.

By the gods, that sound drove him crazy and he didn't think he'd ever tire of hearing it.

Her knees fell to the side as he kissed the curves of her belly and the sweet hollow above her hip bone, while he settled himself between her legs. He pressed his face against her soft inner thighs and parted her slick folds with his tongue. She let out another one of those delicious whimpers when he found her swollen clit and licked it with firm, broad strokes, before slipping a finger into her to tease and coax her closer to orgasm. Burying her hands in his hair, she tilted her hips towards him, her breathing now coming in ragged gasps.

"Do you like that, love?" When he spoke, he did so with his mouth still brushing her skin, knowing the vibration of his voice and his hot breath would add yet another layer of sensations.

"Yes…but you're killing me…you're such a tease." He liked that she was willing to talk, to answer him. Her hips shifted again, as if trying to get him to quicken his pace, though he refused to be rushed.

"I like taking my time, especially since you taste so good and you're so very wet. Wet for me." Lazily, he traced circles around her clit with his tongue, loving how she squirmed below him. He added a second finger and thrust upwards, curling his fingers against her G-spot as he caught her clit between his teeth and teased it.

"Please…" The pleading in her voice reminded him why he loved playing these sorts of games.

"*Please*? Please…*what*? Please stop? Please make me wait until after dinner? Please tie me up and spank me?" He couldn't help but laugh, and damn if it didn't feel good. He'd have plenty of time to feel guilty and miserable later.

"Please…I want to come." She let out a frustrated groan, her hips still squirming under him, her breaths no more than shallow gasps. "I want you to make me come."

Humor laced his voice. "I suppose you've been patient enough."

Sucking her clit into his mouth, he flicked it with his tongue as his fingers flexed and his thrusts quickened until her body tensed and quivered, and she cried out with her release.

If he thought he'd wanted her before, it was nothing compared to the need that was now coursing through him. He nipped at her hip and then kissed the curve of her belly before trailing his way up to her lips. Catching her mouth in a kiss that held all his passion, she wrapped her legs around him and pulled her to him, his cock nudging her upper thigh. It took all the willpower he had to not just plunge into her, unsheathed, especially when her hips kept searching him out.

Condoms...fuck. Did he even have any? And if he did, when had they expired? This was *not* a scenario he'd planned for. Of all the small details to derail an evening.

When a small laugh escaped him, she pulled away to look at him. "What's so funny?"

"I don't suppose you have protection? I...well, I've been living a bit of a solitary life." He stole another kiss, though his hips shifted in protest, as if daring him to throw caution to the wind.

"Maybe. I don't know. I can go have a look, though they might be rather old. I've never done this sort of thing, you know...without protection. But...it's safe on my end, though I get it if you'd rather not..." She shook her head with a smile. "I'm rambling. And it wasn't really something I thought to pack either."

"Are you sure you're okay with this?" He sure as hell hoped she was. After finally taking such a leap, he was desperate to see it through to completion.

She tightened her legs around his hips and kissed him as she ran her hands down his back. "I want you, Aidan. And I trust you. So yeah...I'm sure."

He didn't have to be told twice.

Chapter Four

CHLOE COULD THINK of little else but having Aidan take her, fill her, especially not when she could feel his hard length teasing her. "Please...I want you. Desperately."

How was it that a man she'd only just met could reduce her to begging? She was never like this. *Never.* Hell, she couldn't even remember the last time she'd been with someone, always too busy with work or family.

But now? She'd do just about anything Aidan wanted, even if she didn't quite know why. Maybe it was because Finn was so dear to her, that she felt like she already knew Aidan. Or maybe it was because he was tall, gorgeous, and brilliant. Or maybe it was because he looked so haunted that it broke her heart. But it felt like there was more to it than any of those reasons combined. Maybe it was because from the moment she first set eyes on him, he'd stolen her breath and made her heart race.

With her legs still wrapped around him, she tightened her hold and shifted her hips towards him, hoping he'd show her some mercy. Unable to take much more and hoping it'd spur him on, she bit his neck hard enough to have him cursing under his breath.

His cock slowly parted her slit before he thrust his hips forward and buried himself to the hilt as her body stretched around his generous length and girth. She forced herself to take a breath, for that single thrust nearly had her coming once more. Her clit was already swollen and keeping time with her heartbeat, so each thrust left her teetering, and desperate for more.

He watched her with those sharp hazel eyes, as if not wanting to miss a moment. And yet it made her want to bury her face in his shoulder, her arm, anywhere she might be allowed to escape the scrutiny of his gaze as each thrust pushed her self-control further and further out of her reach.

"You're not to come until I tell you, love. Are we clear?" His stern voice—the authority in it—was nearly her undoing as she teetered on the edge, fighting to hold on. "Answer me, Chloe."

"I'll try." And she would. But how could she promise not to come when she was already so incredibly close?

"Try?" He pulled out of her, leaving her reeling from his absence, though she'd barely had time to protest when he'd flipped her onto her hands and knees, and entered her from behind. He fisted her hair and pulled her head back, but that tiny spark of pain did nothing but push her closer. "Must I really ask again?"

"I won't come until you tell me to...I promise." Though she damn well knew that it was a promise she'd have little control over breaking.

He gripped her hips, his fingers digging in just enough to send a flicker of delicious pain through her body as he thrust into her with such force, it felt like he was not only claiming her body, but her soul. He'd then slowly pull out, ever so slowly, before thrusting back in to claim her once more, indelibly marking her as his.

He draped himself across her back and pinned her to him with an arm across her shoulder, his lips at her ear and his breath warm on her skin. "Can you feel that, love? The way it's building inside you?"

She nodded with a whimper of need, but knew he wanted to hear an answer. How she managed to find the words, she hadn't a clue. "Yes. And I'm so close, Aidan." So fucking close, her head was spinning with the effort to not come.

"I know you are, sweetheart…you're so wet, so tight…and so swollen with need." His words only spurred her on, and she swore she'd never before been left teetering on such a precarious slope. When his pace picked up, each thrust ending on a punctuation, she could take little more.

"Aidan…"

"Will you come for me? Come now, love." He slammed into her as his teeth clamped on her neck, her pain and pleasure mixing to push her over the edge.

She cried out as her body shattered into a million shards of white light, and he joined her with his own release, his hard length pulsing deep inside her and their union complete.

* ❄ *

Chloe wasn't sure what to expect from Aidan, though for now, she was happy enough to just stay curled up in his arms, his warm body tangled with hers. She had to admit that sex with Aidan had been unlike anything she'd ever experienced—not that she'd been with many men, given her crazy work schedule and her non-existent social life. And it had not only been good, but mind-blowing. She wouldn't have pegged herself for the type to like it when a guy took control, and yet…she'd surprised herself.

Unable to resist, she nestled her face in the crook of his neck and kissed him. "You okay?" He'd said very little after their adventure together, and though she knew nothing of his past, she was sure he was going through a rollercoaster of emotions.

"You must be starving." He quickly kissed the top of her head, and shifted her out of his arms before rolling out of bed to grab a pair of sweats and a t-shirt. "The chili should still be hot." Without another word, he made his escape down the stairs.

And that was exactly how it felt—like he was escaping.

She told herself to be understanding. Even if *she* was experiencing a post-orgasmic bliss, it didn't mean he shared her feelings. Though it hurt, she knew he had issues he was struggling with. After all, it'd been three years since he'd last been with anyone. And as good-looking as he was, she was sure he hadn't been celibate all this time because he couldn't find anyone to sleep with him.

Telling herself to pull up her big girl panties and just deal with it, she tossed on his flannel shirt and then padded across the hall to where she'd stashed her bag. It didn't take her long to find her own sweats and a pair of rag wool socks. Though the generator had kicked on and the heat seemed to be working, there was still a bite to the air.

She found him in the kitchen with his back turned to her as he leaned against the counter with his arms outstretched and his head hung low. Though he hadn't said anything to push her away, he felt so incredibly distant, and given how close she'd just felt to him, it was impossible to ignore the growing ache in her chest.

Unsure of what to do to make this better for him, and not wanting to make things worse, she decided to give him a bit of space, and climbed onto a stool. Without a word, he grabbed two bowls from an overhead cabinet and ladled the chili into them, before grabbing some shredded cheese and sour cream. He set a bowl in front of her, along with a spoon and then sat in the other available stool without a word.

"Thanks." She stirred the chili and took a spoonful, but her appetite had soured, and she could barely stand to look at it. She forced a few bites in, knowing she was indeed hungry, and yet she couldn't manage anything more, upset as she was.

"What's wrong?" He barely looked at her between spoonfuls.

She told herself not to say anything. To just let it go. And yet her mouth seemed to have a mind all its own. "What's wrong is that you look miserable. We just had sex and instead of looking happy, you look absolutely wretched. And I get that you have issues you're dealing with, but…" She shook her head with a weary sigh and dropped her spoon in her chili.

"It has nothing to do with you. Okay? Just leave it." He shook his head and shoveled in a bite, his eyes pinned on his meal.

"Yeah…I'll leave it." She shook her head, feeling like a fool as tears stung her eyes. But she would not cry. She refused to show weakness.

It's not like she didn't have her own problems to deal with. This was supposed to be her attempt at a perfect Christmas. Instead, she was stuck on an island with no hope of getting off it before the holidays.

Yet another chance for her to disappoint her father. Yet another chance to not be good enough.

It seemed to be the theme of her life. She told herself she shouldn't care. Told herself none of it mattered. And yet, Aidan only helped to reinforce that thought.

The lights flickered, just as a sob escaped her. Mortified that she was getting so emotional over something that didn't matter, she could think of nothing but escaping to her room when Aidan grabbed her arm and slowly pulled her close.

"Chloe…truly, it's not you. And I'm sorry that I've involved you in any way. I shouldn't have." He ran a hand down her back and then held her close. "I should have known better."

"And by involved, you mean you shouldn't have slept with me." She pulled herself free of his grasp and hopped off the stool. "It's not like I want anything from you, but shit…some common courtesy or manners wouldn't go amiss. Even if you didn't enjoy yourself, you can at least try pretending so that I don't feel like a miserable piece of crap."

"Chloe, stop…" He made a grab for her, but she sidestepped him and bolted for the stairs as her tears finally spilled over. Locking herself in her room, she threw herself on the bed and wondered how the hell it had all gone so terribly wrong.

How foolish was she that she was letting this get to her? She knew what she was getting into when she decided to sleep with Aidan, though she supposed she'd expected a few blissful days of hanging out while the blizzard raged. Getting the cold shoulder moments after sleeping with him hadn't exactly factored into her snowed-in fantasy.

It didn't help that she was emotionally on edge to begin with, since she really had been hoping for a perfect Christmas with her family. It would be one more opportunity for her father to give her that look of his...the one that said she'd tried but didn't quite live up to his expectations. That she hadn't managed things as well as her mother had, and she wasn't as successful as her two brothers, and she'd only thought of herself when it came to going to college.

Just one big disappointment. Never quite managing to measure up.

And she knew better than to pay it any heed. She *knew* she was better than what her father—or Aidan—saw in her. She had a good life, and was a good sister and daughter, even if her father refused to see it. So then, why was she always trying to convince him of that? Why the hell was she wasting her time and energy when he'd only ever see what he wanted to?

Feeling chilled, she crawled under the blankets and snuggled in, while vowing to stay positive and not let things get to her. She couldn't live her life trying to please others—her father and Aidan included. All she could do is try to live her life by her own moral code, and hope she measured up to her own expectations.

As for Aidan, she hadn't been expecting much, but...what the hell? Well, lesson learned. He got to scratch his three-year itch before turning back into the grumpy bastard who'd answered the door when she first turned up. It'd been fun while it lasted, but she'd be damned if she'd be going down that road anytime soon, if that was going to be his reaction.

Once was more than enough and quite frankly, she didn't need that sort of complication in her life. If he didn't want her or want anything to do with her, then she'd get out of his hair and out of his way.

The Siren Song Inn might not be open for business, but she was sure there were other places to stay, like a bed and breakfast. So that was exactly what she'd do. If Aidan wanted to be left alone, then she'd grant him his wish.

Chapter Five

AFTER SPENDING A restless night tossing and turning, Aidan finally pulled himself out of bed, though he was far from ready to face the day. It was the day before Christmas, and that meant this was the worst day of the year. The day his life had forever changed.

As if this day couldn't get any worse on its own, he now had the added guilt of being an ass to Chloe. It'd been a mistake to sleep with her when, emotionally, he was in no shape to do so. He should regret it. And yet he didn't.

All she'd really done is try to help him out and be accommodating. And she hadn't asked for anything in return. And yet, instead of finding a way to be more sensitive, more respectful of her and the good time they'd shared, he'd let his bad mood take over and make him miserable.

He took a quick shower to help wake himself up, and then got dressed before taking a peek out the window. The snow hadn't let up one bit. If anything, it seemed to be coming down even harder, blanketing everything and blocking out the sun.

He knew he'd have to make it up to Chloe for being a jerk, though he hadn't a clue as to how to go about it. It was going to be a hard enough day as it was, and he didn't need her to be miserable with him, too. The door to her room was open, but she wasn't there. Nor was she downstairs.

What the hell? Where was she?

Paisley trotted behind him as he went through the house, calling out her name. When he turned up empty, panic seeped into his chest as he expanded his search for her. He went out his front door and was relieved to see that at least she hadn't taken her car anywhere, though she'd moved it down towards the barn. It was a small SUV and likely had all-wheel drive, but with more than two feet of snow, he didn't care what she was driving—it wasn't safe.

Hannah's accident flashed into his mind—an icy road late at night, pieces of her car scattered everywhere, the cop lights blinding him, and strong arms holding him back as he struggled to get to her.

But this wasn't Hannah. It was Chloe.

Suddenly he was desperate to find her, and needed to make sure she was safe. There…footsteps from her car to the barn. They'd been blown away by the fierce winds, but he could still make out their faint outline. How long ago had she left the house?

He raced over and pulled open the door, immediately spotting her. She was asleep in an office chair with her head on the desk he'd built for her father. His pulse finally started to slow as a wave of relief washed over him.

He ran his hand over her dark hair and bent over to kiss her cheek and found her ice cold, his pulse racing once more as he tried not to panic. She must have come out here in the middle of the night. And for what? Why? She could have frozen to death. The barn might have protected her from the winds, but it wasn't heated unless he was running the wood stove.

Squatting at her side, he gave her a gentle shake to try to wake her. "Come on, love. We need to get you inside. Get you out of the cold."

She started to stir and come to, but she still seemed drowsy and Aidan knew he had to get her warm. He scooped her into his arms as she mumbled and her head lolled around before settling against his shoulder. Still holding her, he fumbled with his key, but managed to get the door unlocked to the passage way. He got her settled in front of the fireplace and quickly got the fire going to try to warm her. Once he'd built the fire up, he added several more logs until it was blazing.

There wasn't a hospital on the island, though if need be, he could get the sheriff to open the bridge and take Chloe to the one on the mainland. Was the doctor even on the island, or had he gone to see his daughter in Portland?

He needed to get her warmed up but wasn't sure what'd be best. Keeping her dry in front of the fire with the blankets piled on her? Stripping both of them down and trying to warm her skin to skin? Or maybe he should try the hot tub?

She shook her head as if trying to clear it from a fog. "What happened?" Her words were spoken as if mumbled through pea soup.

He wanted to yell and scream at her. Tell her she'd nearly gotten herself killed. That she'd scared him half to death. Instead, he took a deep breath and brushed her dark hair from her pale, cold skin. "You were in the barn. What the hell were you doing there?"

"I was going to try to get the desk in my car and then go to a local bed and breakfast. I found one online, so I emailed them last night... didn't want to be in your way here. But the desk was too heavy." Another shake of her head. "And the roads...there was so much snow."

"Exactly! The roads aren't passable, Chloe—not even for driving around the island. And then what the hell were you thinking you'd do? Drive yourself into the ocean? Wrap your car around a tree?" Unbelievable. She could've gotten herself killed. "You're staying here until this storm blows over. Do you hear me? It's not up for debate. And we still need to get you warmed up. Why you didn't come back into the house is beyond me…"

"The doors…they locked behind me. I didn't realize…"

Just as he was getting ready to yell at her about not ringing the god-damned doorbell, she drifted back to sleep, her body still too cold to waste energy with remaining conscious. And then he wondered if she had actually tried to wake him, since he usually slept like the dead. She likely had pounded and rang the bell repeatedly without any luck.

With a weary sigh, he took another look at her. Her breathing was good. He just needed to get her warm as quickly as possible.

She could yell at him when she was conscious again—because he was about to get them both naked, without her permission. He got himself undressed first and then made quick work of her clothing, with only the fleeting thought that this was far different than the first time he'd tackled the task. It made his heart ache with regret and frustration. Though she did stir a bit, she only mumbled a handful of words before going quiet once more.

The sofa was pretty wide and could accommodate both of them, especially since they'd be pressed together to try to warm her. He slipped in behind her so she'd still get the heat from the fire, and then tried his best to cover as much of her as possible with his own body.

Bloody hell, she was cold. Damn cold. He suppressed a shiver and held her to him, while trying to reconcile the events that led up to their current predicament. He knew it'd been because he was an ass, and his actions had harmed another, yet again.

It was why he lived alone and seldom dealt with people. So he could rage and hate himself without subjecting others to it. Without putting others in harm's way. Once again, he should have paid closer attention, been more considerate, seen the signs. Yet he was too selfish, too absorbed in his own problems to see what was happening around him.

He wondered if he'd ever learn. Clearly not, if Chloe was any indication.

He'd just have to try to make it up to her. Because, truth be told, Chloe had actually made him feel more human—more like the person he'd been before Hannah's accident. She'd made him smile, made him laugh, and even made him forget his demons, if for a short while.

He felt a small spark of hope ignite in his heart, so precious and delicate that it'd take very little to snuff it out of existence if he wasn't careful. The darkness within told him he didn't deserve hope or happiness—not when Hannah was in her grave, and their unborn child never got to take its first breath. Even Chloe had ended up in danger after a mere day in his presence. Yet, his night with Chloe—and nearly losing her—reminded him of what it felt like to be alive.

He may not deserve happiness, but he was damn near exhausted of hating life and himself.

❋ ❋ ❋

Having drifted off into a light slumber, Aidan awoke when Chloe started to stir in his arms. Her eyes flickered open, and though she took a minute to focus her gaze, her eyes seemed clear, though still heavy with sleep.

"Hey…" A lazy smile slipped onto her lips as she slowly closed her eyes again, nestling lower in his embrace, everything about her moving at a languid pace.

He wanted to shake her awake, just so he could make sure that she was fine and hadn't suffered any ill effects. But with relief washing over him, he instead kissed the top of her head and tightened his hold on her, debating whether or not he'd ever let her go.

The thought caught him off guard. Normally he'd balk at such a thing, but this time around, he found himself remarkably at ease with the idea.

"You really had me scared there, Chloe." He was even taken aback by his admission to her. "You were so cold...I can't bear to think of what might have happened if I hadn't found you when I did."

Given how much he'd tossed and turned early on in the night, he could have easily slept for several more hours by the time he did finally fall into a deep sleep. He didn't want to think of the condition he'd have found her in if he'd awoken much later than he had.

When she shifted again to get comfortable, his body became acutely aware of her lush curves and how they molded to his body, not to mention the tiny detail of them both being naked. Wanting her had never come into the equation when he'd been so worried about her. But now that she seemed to be doing fine, his need for her seemed to overrule his other sensibilities.

And she must have noticed.

She lifted her head off his shoulder and looked up at him with a curious look he couldn't quite pinpoint. "We're naked." It was as if she'd just realized it.

"Indeed we are—though before you get upset with me, I only did it to try to get you warm. Skin on skin, and all that..." He groaned, sounding like an idiot.

She let out a sigh. "Well, if that's the only reason, then it's a damn shame."

He pulled back as if he'd misunderstood, thought about asking her to repeat herself, and then let it go with a laugh. Forward indeed. "You need to regain your strength. And what sort of jerk would I be if I took advantage of you when you were barely conscious?"

She kissed the hollow of his neck just above his collarbone, her lips soft and warm, and sending a spike of need through to his core. "I'm conscious now."

"And you still need to rest and try to stay warm." He should cook them breakfast, too—even if it was already past lunch time. She could probably do with a refuel after her body had expended so much energy to keep her from freezing.

Her hips shifted against his hard cock, reminding him of how much time he had to make up for. "Sweetheart…I'm trying to be good, but you're not making it easy on me."

She nudged him until he shifted onto his back, and then slipped a leg around his waist so she could lie down on top of him. "See…you're keeping me warm just fine."

With his cock trapped between the two of them and her slick heat pressed up against his hard length, he couldn't help but run his hands down her back to grip her ass. "What I see is that your ass cheeks are like blocks of ice."

"Then maybe you should heat them up for me. Or…you could go in search of something warmer." She shifted her body up and down his entire length until he lost nearly all semblance of control. "Then again, there's also something to be said about friction, since it seems to do a pretty damn good job, too."

"Chloe…you're killing me here." Here he was trying to do the caring and chivalrous thing of not attacking her before she was fully recovered, and she was making it nearly impossible for him to say no.

"May I?" Her words danced over his skin as she nuzzled him and kissed his neck. She may not have been terribly specific, but he knew exactly what she was asking by the way her body shifted against his with her slick heat slipping along his length.

The fact that she was asking for permission when she could so easily just take him, nearly did him in. When he spoke, his voice was thick with need. "What is it you want, love? Tell me."

She let out a small moan in protest, but didn't elaborate further or answer his question. He knew it wasn't always easy to verbalize such things or own up to one's needs and desires. Yet speaking the words out loud, especially to another person, meant claiming that part of yourself, and that could be empowering. "I'm still waiting for an answer, sweetheart. Come on…you can tell me. You know I'll happily oblige you."

Another moan of protest, and this time she punctuated it by biting his neck and tilting her hips against him to increase the friction between them. "But you know what I want."

"And you know that I want to hear you say it. Now, sweetheart. Before I insist that you give me every detail, all while looking me in the eyes." Though he couldn't see her face since she'd buried it at his neck, he knew her cheeks must be blushing furiously. He supposed that was one way to warm her up.

She looked up at him with a glare, and the humor in her voice made him smile. "You're a real pain in the ass. You know that, right?"

"That can be arranged too, if it's what you want." When she playfully swatted at him, he couldn't help but laugh—and damn if it didn't feel good. "Well? I'm still waiting."

He kissed her cheek, her jawline, her neck, loving how she arched up to give him easy access, as if offering herself to him, to do as he wished. A needy little moan escaped her, though it was laced with frustration. "*Fine.* Fine. I want you…your cock…in me."

"Is that all?" His kisses wandered down her neck to the slope of her shoulder, as his hands went to her hips and, with a small lift, seated her onto his hard length. Her exhale was so full of satisfaction and contentment, he couldn't help but laugh. "Better?"

"Yes…*sooo* much better." She rolled her hips along his shaft as he sat up and caught her nipple, first one and then the other, sucking and nipping as her movements quickened.

He picked up his pace, thrusting up from under her, even as he pulled the blankets up over her shoulders. He was still worried about her getting chilled, and wasn't convinced their current activities wouldn't set her recovery back. Not that he could stop now, even if he wanted to.

She was so tight, so slick—so fucking gorgeous—it left his head spinning and had him wondering if he'd ever get his fill of her. It seemed she'd walked right into his life and, like a whirlwind, turned everything he knew on its head. The thought that the storm would eventually blow over and she'd soon be leaving left him wondering if he might be able to convince her to come back for a visit. Or maybe he should ask her to stay...

He kissed her, letting his tongue play over hers, as he took all she had to offer. He didn't know how much longer he'd be able to hold out, and he knew with the pace they were setting and with the eager whimpers she couldn't quite contain, she wasn't going to last long either.

She grew tight around him as he gripped her hips in his tight grasp, their pace growing frenzied. "Come for me. Now, love."

And she did—her body shuddering against him as she cried out and he joined her in his release, his cock pumping into her until he was spent and there was nothing but the two of them, the rest of the world falling away.

Chapter Six

CHLOE TRIED NOT to get defensive as Aidan questioned her about trying to leave the night before. He was still holding her close, which certainly helped matters, but she really didn't want to explain to him the reason why it was so important that she get the chance to spend the holidays with her family. Not that she'd be going anywhere with the storm still raging.

"I didn't want to be in your way. I know you're not used to company—Finn said you liked your privacy. And then we'd argued, and you were looking so miserable...I just figured I'd grab the desk and go. I'd spend the night at the B&B, and then see if I could get off the island. Maybe speak to the police about opening the bridge." She snuggled deeper into his embrace, her head propped against his chest.

"Firstly, they don't open that bridge for anyone, unless it's an actual emergency—and I'm talking medical, life-or-death stuff. But even if you made it off the island, the roads are still dangerous, Chloe." He shook his head, but there was also a tension and annoyance in him that she hadn't expected. "I get that you want to spend the holidays with your family, but for fuck's sake, you need to keep yourself safe, first and foremost."

"Yeah, I know…" And she did. Sort of. If it was anything else, she'd have no problem canceling her plans, but the fact that she'd be disappointing her father—yet again—left her frustrated and miserable. She shouldn't care. She was always going out of her way to take care of her family, and yet it never quite seemed enough. "It's just one of those family things. My father…"

"The one the desk's for…" He sat up just enough to look at her, though the intensity of his gaze had her pulling away. "Seems like you're really going out of your way for him."

"It's complicated." She distracted herself with the blanket, running her fingers along the lines of the plaid, trying to avoid looking at him while she spoke. "My mom's gone, so he's alone and…I'm the oldest. My two brothers were really young at the time and my dad needed help."

"So you essentially stepped into the role of your mother to help raise them." He ran a gentle hand down her back, and then pulled her in close. "How old were you when she passed?"

"Fourteen." Far too young to deal with losing a parent, and yet those were the cards fate had dealt her, and there was no giving them back.

"I can't imagine taking on such responsibility at that age." He let out a ragged sigh and held her to him as she tried to push away the memories. "I can see why you've been wanting to get home, but you know he'll be understanding. Especially when it's out of your control."

"What he'll be is disappointed—*again*." The moment the words were out of her mouth, she regretted speaking them out loud. "I'm sorry. I shouldn't have said anything."

She tried to pull away, wanting nothing more than to escape to her room and bury herself under the blankets, because she knew Aidan wasn't going to let this go. She'd do anything to end this discussion, and as if sensing she might bolt, he tightened his hold.

"Wait...what do you mean, he'll be disappointed?" He looked at her as if he couldn't quite grasp the concept. "You can't really mean that. Are you sure you're not just reading into it?"

She took it as an out, even if she knew it wasn't the truth. "I'm sure I am." She managed a smile, though she knew she was a horrible liar.

"You really do think he's disappointed in you..." His eyes narrowed in disbelief and with a simmering anger. "I just don't understand how that could happen. Did something happen?"

She shrugged. "I was selfish—I put myself first when it came to college. I could have gone to a local community school, but instead I went out to the Berkshires and that meant leaving them behind to fend for themselves."

"And by fend for themselves, you mean an adult man and two teen-age boys would have to make do without you to take care of them." His brows were raised, his jaw was tight, and he was *not happy*.

"It wasn't just for school. It was work, too...I left for Boston. Got a job straight out of college. But I send them money. I go and visit. I try." She cupped his cheek and kissed him, hoping it'd ease the tension that was pouring off him in waves. He had his own problems to deal with and she didn't need to add to them.

"Sounds to me like you not only try, but do more than your share. Not that he sees it. Am I right?" He slowly shook his head, his hazel eyes burning with anger. "And you've likely been bending over back-wards so he won't be disappointed."

"It doesn't matter, Aidan. Honestly." She just had to live her life— *her* life, not the one her father wanted for her. "I'm an adult and I make my own decisions. I'm okay with that."

He cupped the back of her neck and pulled her close, kissing her head. "Of course you are, love. I just hate to see you killing yourself so as not to disappoint him, when it sounds to me like it doesn't matter what you do."

"If I moved back home…" Not that she would.

"Do you really think that would make him happy? Or would he just move on to the next thing on his list? Something new to be disappointed in. Because people like that aren't ever happy, love." He cupped her face in his hands and held her gaze. "And you deserve so much better than that."

She gave him a shrug and let him hold her in his strong arms. "Unfortunately, we don't always get what we deserve."

※ ❄ ※

Chloe leaned back against Aidan as they sat in front of the fire. Though she was no longer feeling the effects of nearly freezing her butt off, Aidan had insisted she stay put, even as he got them leftover chili for dinner and made her fireplace s'mores for dessert.

"Thanks for all this…you've been really sweet to me." And he had been, even though his mood had grown sullen as the day trickled into the evening.

"It's the least I can do after being such a jerk last night." He ran a finger down her cheek and then settled back against the sofa with a sigh.

"You weren't the only one at fault. I read too much into it, Aidan. I think I was being overly sensitive because of my own problems." She linked her hand with his, wanting some sort of connection between them, since it felt like he was drifting further and further away with each passing moment. "Aidan…I hope you know that I'm here for you if you want to talk. I don't know what sort of demons you're struggling with, but…"

"My demons are my own to deal with, Chloe. There's nothing anyone can do to fix my problems." As if punctuating his hurt and anger, the winds howled away as branches beat against the house. "*You* can't fix this—and you can't fix me. Are we clear?"

"Yeah…crystal." She told herself not to let it bother her. He was upset, and it wasn't because of her or anything she'd done, but rather because of things that were outside of their control. And yet it hurt that he was pushing her away.

Part of her felt foolish for thinking that he might open up to her after she'd told him about her family and their problems. She knew better. And yet she was quickly realizing that the reason she'd expected him to let her in on his troubles was because she was reading far more into whatever it was that they were doing. She had stupidly started to fall for him, when he was *not* emotionally available.

He cursed under his breath. "I know I'm being an asshole, Chloe. But it's who I am—and you deserve better than that, even if you only have to put up with me for a few days. I just can't be anything else. And for that, I'm sorry."

"You're not an asshole. I just stupidly thought…" When her eyes started to sting, she was thankful that they didn't have many lights on as they sat by the fire.

"You thought what? That this would turn into some happily ever after?" He scoffed and shook his head. Though his words stung, she could hear the hurt in his voice. "Well, it's not going to happen. I live in a nightmare—not some goddamned fairytale. And the last thing I'm going to do is drag you down with me."

"So it's perfectly fine for us to discuss *my* issues and problems, but your issues are off-limits. Instead, I get to just sit idly by and watch your mood sour with each passing minute, so I'm left thinking I'd rather brave a blizzard than stay here and feel miserable." And she would, because the longer she stayed here, the more unbearable it got. She couldn't bear to see him hurting. It was killing her.

"You're going nowhere, Chloe. It's not even up for discussion. Do you hear me?" He may have been in a bad mood before, but right now he was downright furious with her.

Well, she had a temper too, and though she was trying to stay reasonable, she refused to let him push her around. "That's not a decision you get to make on my behalf. I'm not saying I'm going anywhere, since I know the roads are impossible to navigate, but whether I come or go is *my* choice and mine alone."

His lips curled up in a smug smile that still carried his anger with it. "Sweetheart, I'd have you locked in my room before I let you go out in that storm."

"Oh, sure…why don't you just cuff me to your bed while you're at it?" She was furious and got up to go, though he was quick on her heels. If she thought she'd be able to get away from him, she was gravely mistaken.

He pulled her into his arms and held her close, her body pinned to his as he nipped at her neck, his breath hot on her skin. "Don't tempt me, sweetheart. You'd be a fine sight tied to my bed."

She did her best to ignore the shiver of need that raced through her, her body's reaction to him—to his words—instantaneous, especially when her memories of their coupling were still so vivid in her mind. "Just because you have bucket loads of money and are used to people letting you be a grump does *not* mean I have to put up with it. Even if I am trapped in this house with you."

The lights flickered off and then on as she growled out a cry of frustration over everything and pulled out of his grasp. She cursed herself for getting emotional and letting any of this bother her. As soon as the storm blew over, she'd be gone, and he'd be nothing but a memory and a heartache.

"Do you think this is easy for me? Do you think I just woke up one morning and decided to close myself off from the world? Well, I didn't, Chloe. I had my life stolen from me. Turned upside down."

"Then let me be here for you. For fuck's sake, Aidan—let me in. There's no reason to go through this alone." Her anger was turning to sorrow, and it left her heart breaking for him. Yet there was little she could do for him if he didn't trust her enough to open up to her. "I've seen glimpses of what you're like when you're happy…and I want that for you. I don't know what happened, but you have to let it go. You can't let it consume you."

He just hung his head looking so defeated, she couldn't help but forget her anger with him. "That's just it…I don't deserve to be happy. Not when…"

She slipped her arms around his waist and held him tightly, wondering when he'd managed to claim her heart. "Everyone deserves a bit of happiness, Aidan. I don't know what happened to make you think otherwise, but you're mistaken. I know I haven't known you long, but I don't need years to figure out that you're a good man."

"No—what I am is a greedy and self-centered man." He pulled away from her and started to pace, his body tense with anger and hurt, his face contorted by the pain. "I was too busy to give a shit about what was happening around me, and others paid the price. Two lives…" His voice cracked then, as did her heart. "And their blood is on *my* hands. That's something I'll have to live with the rest of my life."

Chapter Seven

AIDAN PULLED AWAY from Chloe, his memories of that night too much to bear. And yet she refused to go, forcing him to face her and to face his demons. She pulled him onto the sofa and held him against her so there was no escape, his only option but to give in and hold her back.

"I need you to tell me what happened, because I refuse to believe any of what you've said. It may only be days since we first met, but I swear, I know you well enough, and I cannot imagine you causing anyone's death on purpose." Her body pressed against him, offering him a warm haven as her sweet scent filled his head and took the edge off his nightmare. "Let me help, Aidan. I care too much about you, and it's killing me to see you suffering like this on your own. Please… let me in."

The words stuck in his throat, and yet he found himself wanting to tell her, if only to convince her of the monster he truly was. Maybe then she'd keep her distance and stay away before he hurt her too. He took a deep breath and held it until his lungs burned before finally letting it out. "I don't even know where to start…"

She nuzzled up against him and kissed his neck as he held her to him. "Just start from the beginning, love. I'm here for you."

He let his memories wander, letting them play out like snapshots and clips of his life. He saw not only his brownstone in the Back Bay of Boston, his offices and their labs in Cambridge where he got his start, but the tiny Cambridge apartment.

And he saw Hannah.

"We'd met just as I was starting up my tech company. There was a pub not far from where I'd set up my lab and where she worked. Hannah…" He let out a ragged breath, thinking how different she was from Chloe with her honey blonde hair and bronzed skin. Both women beautiful, but so different from each other. "I was still dirt poor at the time, but she didn't mind. Every moment that I wasn't working, we seemed to spend together. And we were damn happy. But then things started to change—and we thought it was for the better."

Chloe listened quietly and said little, letting him tell his story at his pace. And for that he was grateful. "My company started to do really well and I went from making very little to making more money than I could've ever imagined. But that meant we not only needed to stay ahead of the competition, we also needed to keep our clients happy. Hannah tried to be understanding about the long hours I worked, and she really was at the beginning. But things didn't let up."

It was the start of his demise. "I figured that if I couldn't give her my time, the least I could do is let her enjoy herself. We bought a gorgeous townhouse, she quit her job, and I let her buy whatever would make her happy. Except…"

"Except that it wasn't really a substitute for your absence." She let out a sigh as he ran a hand down her back.

"No, I suppose it wasn't. I did propose and she accepted, but my hours didn't improve. The more I was gone, the more she started to change, though I wasn't ever there to notice. Her buying habits started to get more extreme and when I was too busy working late, she was happy to go out and have a good time without me." He shook his head and squeezed his eyes shut for a long moment, trying his best to push away the worst of his memories so he could continue.

"I didn't realize that her drinking had become excessive or that she was starting to dabble in recreational drugs. But I had deadlines and a company to run, and I didn't have the time to do more than call her to let her know I'd be late. We'd argue about it, with her demanding more of my time, and me insisting that it just wasn't feasible with my workload. So instead she'd go out without me—new friends, new bars, anything to keep herself busy." He continued now, the words refusing to be contained when the end was so near. "The holidays were approaching and she made me promise that I'd go to this Christmas Eve party one of her new friends was throwing. I swore to her that we'd go, even though I was swamped."

His heart felt like it was going to leap out of his chest. He could barely breathe, and yet he somehow managed to continue. "There was a last-minute problem with a client and instead of leaving it until after the holidays, I told Hannah to go on without me and I'd meet her there. Except that it took me longer to wrap things up than I'd originally estimated. By the time I'd left to go to the party, she was already on her way home, and since I'd been stuck in the lab all day, I hadn't even realized that the weather had taken a turn for the worse."

He swallowed against the lump in his throat as it all played out in front of him, as if he were living through it once more. "It was snowing but with a freezing rain added to the mix. And she'd been drinking because she'd expected me to show up to drive her home— and because she'd been drinking far too much in general. Of course, I was too busy to bother showing up on time and I didn't get to her until it was far too late. She was a block from our house when she hit a patch of black ice while taking a turn. Her car hit a telephone pole, and…she hadn't been wearing her seat belt."

"Oh, Aidan…" Chloe held him to her, but he wasn't done.

"The ambulance and the police…the lights…I was on my way home to find her when I came across the accident. They tried to keep me from going to her. Said it was already too late. And it was. I should have been there to take her home. I should have paid more attention not just to her, but to what was happening. And that wasn't even the end of it. A week later, the autopsy report came in. She'd been seven weeks pregnant. We were going to have a baby."

He'd have wept for his loss, though his tears seemed to have run dry after so many years. Now all he had was pain and anger.

And yet Chloe had tears for him. So he held her as she shed tears for his loss, though he could offer her little comfort.

✻ ❄ ✻

Aidan didn't know how long they'd stayed that way, with her laying there in his arms. The fire had started to die down, and he half wondered if she'd eventually cried herself to sleep.

He'd kept his story locked up so tightly in his memory and trapped in his soul that he hadn't even thought himself capable of telling her what happened. He was sure that letting Chloe into his nightmare would do nothing but rip open his wounds. Yet…he found that the pain strangling his heart had eased just a little.

What he found most surprising, however, was that by letting go of some of his pain, his heart was able to let something else take root. He couldn't quite say if it was love or just hope, but something inside him had changed and Chloe had given him a gift he hadn't expected. A chance to heal and maybe someday find happiness once more.

As if sensing him stir, she touched her lips to his neck in a whisper of a kiss, and then another, before nestling against him. "Aidan…" When she spoke, he could still hear the worry and pain in his voice, even though her words were merely a whisper. "I know you feel responsible for what happened, but you must know that what happened…it's not your fault."

He ran a hand over her hair and kissed the top of her head, needing to feel her close. "It was my fault that I didn't see what was happening right under my nose. She was my fiancée, and instead of tending to her needs, I handed her a credit card and tried to buy her happiness. And I should have been there to drive her home."

"I know, love. But…she was also responsible for her own actions. She didn't have to drink and party to pass the time, and she didn't have to drive herself home that night." He started to tense as his anger simmered, but she held onto him and forced him to listen to her. "You can get angry with me if you want, but I'm telling you now that this was not your fault, even if it doesn't lessen the tragedy of it."

"I should have been there."

"And I know that will haunt you until your dying days, but it's still not your fault, love." She cupped his face in her hands and forced him to look at her. "It's not. And it's killing me to see you blaming yourself."

"Chloe, please…I can't deal with this just now." After so many years of beating himself up, he was too weary to argue with her or discuss it any further. And he didn't want to be reminded that this was Christmas Eve. All he wanted was to find comfort and oblivion in her arms. "Will you come to bed with me?"

She kissed him in response, a kiss that was both sweet and passionate, and so full of emotion. He could happily lose himself in her and forget all his problems—if only his demons would let him.

He led her to his room as they quickly rid themselves of their clothing, one kiss moving into the next, as if they couldn't bear to be apart for more than a moment's breath. Unlike the heated and frenzied couplings they'd had thus far, they came together this time like lovers who knew each other, the intimacy between them easing his pain further. Though it'd been three years since Hannah's death, he now realized that perhaps he'd lost her well before that. And that only strengthened his connection to Chloe.

As the snow continued to rage outside, he held her close and trailed kisses down the length of her neck. Nestling himself between her legs, he took her in one go, desperate to be joined with her, as if she could keep him anchored in the present. Wrapping her legs around him, she pulled him close as he slowly thrust into her, his body gliding up against hers as he filled her, took her, claimed her—just as she claimed his heart.

He gathered up both her wrists in one of his large hands and held them firmly above her head as he let his other hand slip over her skin to cup her breast and pinch her nipple. She tightened around his cock in response, all sweet tension and soft curves. A body he'd never tire of exploring.

Needy whimpers escaped her sweet lips as her hips eagerly tilted up to meet him, her pace quickening as she neared her release and he pushed her over the edge. He stifled a groan as his pleasure and need unfurled deep within him, his orgasm curling around hers, his breathing heavy as he held her body to his, stealing just one more kiss.

With her still in his arms, he nestled her in at his side, feeling more content than he had in years. And yet…he knew that this was temporary. The storm would eventually blow out to sea, and she'd pack up her desk and go.

Precarious as his newfound happiness was, he knew he'd slip back into the darkness once she was gone. But there was more to it than that. Truth was, he liked her—and he liked having her around. Liked how he felt about himself when she was close. Liked that he now had a sense of hope.

He took a deep breath to steady his nerves and to find the courage he'd need to get the words out. "I want you to stay, Chloe."

"I am staying, love. It'll still be days before the storm blows over." She gently trailed kisses down his neck and across his chest. "Unless that's a problem. I know you weren't exactly happy about me getting stuck here."

"No, sweetheart. That's not what I meant." He'd been such an ass to her. He'd never get her to agree. "I want you to move to Mermaid Isle. Or you could move in here with me, if you'd prefer."

She propped herself up enough to look at him, her brow furrowed in confusion. "Aidan…you barely know me. You can't really mean that. And I have a job. In Boston."

It was easy enough to know those would be her exact words since any logical and sane person would have had those exact same thoughts. And yet he didn't care. "I do know you, Chloe. And I know this sounds insane. But I mean every word of what I just said."

"I can't just quit my job, Aidan. My family depends on the money I send. I mean…I do pretty well for myself, and so I'm able to send a decent amount. But I've also busted my butt to get my promotions." She shook her head and looked at him with such pained sadness, as she cupped his cheek and stole a kiss. "I just can't."

"Your work…is it what you love to do? Is it what you're most passionate about? Or is there something else you'd rather be doing?" She must know money wasn't an issue for him.

"Yeah, of course there's other stuff I'd rather be doing. I'd love to be a potter, but that's not realistic—and I can't just let you pay my way. I'm not going to be some paid mistress or girlfriend, just because you have money to burn." She sat up out of his arms. "I have no interest in your billions and I can take care of myself."

"Let me hire you then." Seemed like a simple enough solution, and once he set his mind to something, he was determined to make it happen. "I need someone to help me with my carpentry orders."

"Then you need an assistant—and that's not me." She cupped his face and kissed him. "You know I like you—way too much—but my career is my only safety net, and I can't just throw it all away. What happens six months from now when you get bored of me?"

She didn't quite get it, though he couldn't blame her for not understanding, when things were only now starting to solidify in his own head. "I could never bore of you, sweetheart, though I understand why you're hesitant. And I'll do whatever it takes to make you realize this is the best thing, not only for me, but for you. I'd even move back to Boston if it meant being with you."

"There's no way I can let you do that, Aidan. And I'll happily come and visit, but I don't want your money. I just couldn't. I couldn't bear to have you thinking that's the reason I'm with you, or that I'm staying because of some monetary arrangement. It belittles the way I feel about you." She scoffed and gave her head a slow shake. "And don't ask me how that happened, but I do have feelings for you, even if it's been mere days."

He pulled her close and rolled them over as she laughed, switching their positions so she was now underneath him. He stole a quick kiss with a smile. "Sweetheart, that makes me a happy man. Except for the fact that you'd rather not see me at all—or only see me on occasion—rather than make us both happy and move in with me. And that's all so that I don't think you're after my money. You realize how silly that sounds, right?"

She swatted at him playfully. "It's not silly. Though I suppose I could look for work in Portland. I'd be closer, at least."

By the gods, she was stubborn. But he'd make her see sense, even if it took all day. "You do realize the sort of leap this is for me, right?"

"I know it is." She nipped at his bottom lip and then kissed him.

"Then do it for me, Chloe. Please." He saw her determination waver just a little, so he pressed on. "I'll pay for your brothers' college loans, pay your father's mortgage, whatever it is that you feel is keeping you at your job. And then you can do what you've always wanted to do. You'd mentioned pottery, right? Well then, let me set you up with a studio. You can live here and sell your art in town and at the local galleries for money. I have plenty of connections, since I occasionally sell my own pieces."

"I can't take your money, Aidan. But...things aren't as bad now that Stephen and Jack have graduated and found decent jobs." She shook her head with a sigh. "And what if you get tired of me? What then?"

"I could never tire of you, love. You just need to trust me, and know that I'll make things right between us." He brushed a stray curl from her face, his heart so full of love and hope. "What do you say? Please...say you'll at least give it a try. For me."

She let out a sigh, but it was followed by a smile. "All right then. I suppose we can do a trial period. But I make no promises."

"None at all, love."

Chapter Eight

CHLOE AWOKE TO find herself nestled comfortably in Aidan's strong arms, while the sun streamed in through the windows. As if sensing that she'd awoken, he pulled her close and kissed the top of her head while she snuggled against his warm and muscular body. "Looks like the storm finally blew out to sea."

"Merry Christmas, sweetheart." He nuzzled her, his thick stubble rough against her cheeks and then kissed her slow and sweet before giving her a smile that stole her heart.

"Merry Christmas." She cupped his face and lost herself in those intelligent hazel eyes of his. "You know, you've got a damn sexy smile. It lights up your eyes like magic."

He brushed his thumb over her cheek, his touch gentle though his fingers were a little rough from his woodworking. "I hope you realize that it's because of you that I'm able to smile again. I know it's far from being over, but for the first time I feel like I might actually be able to crawl out of this darkness."

"Well then, you'll need to consider that your Christmas gift since I haven't exactly had the chance to get you anything." Who knew things would have turned out this way? All because a storm zigged when it should have zagged.

"I couldn't have asked for anything better, love. Not that I have any sort of gift for you either. Unless, of course..." He kissed her cheek and then her neck as his large hands palmed her butt cheeks and pulled her up against his morning erection.

"*Oh*...That could definitely work." Her body came alive under his touch, her pulse skipping a beat as it echoed between her legs where she was still pleasantly sore from their adventures of the last few days. She reached down between them and wrapped her fingers around his wide girth to stroke him, the feel of him so silky smooth and warm, and yet steely hard just below the surface.

"By the gods, woman, that feels too damn good, especially after going without for so long. But..." He covered her hand with his to stop her. "I have a favor to ask you."

Suddenly, he was looking rather serious, sending a flicker of worry through her. "Sure. What is it?"

"My entire family usually gets together for Christmas and..." He shook his head and looked away. "I haven't spent the holiday with them in years now, and they're only forty minutes away. I think they'd be really happy if we showed up for a visit. And Finn will be there."

Oh, boy. Though she knew Finn, she wasn't sure about meeting the rest of his family, especially when things were moving rather quickly between her and Aidan. The last thing she wanted was for them to think she was dating their son for the money—and with her new plans to move in mere days after meeting him, she wouldn't blame them if they were suspicious of her. "I don't know how good an idea that is. And the bridge is still closed, right?"

"They only keep it closed while the storms are raging. I suspect it won't be long before they open and plow it." He brushed a stray lock of hair from her face.

"Or we could just stay in your cozy bed and have sex all day." Her hand found his cock once more, hoping to stage a convincing argument. "Pretty please? With sugar on top?"

"Sweetheart…that's all too tempting an idea."

"Maybe you should go alone. After all these years, I'm sure they're going to want you to themselves. And really, I'm fine just hanging out at your place. I could keep Paisley company. We could have a girls' day in."

Chloe wasn't convinced this was a good idea. Mere days earlier, Aidan hadn't even known her. And now, he wanted her to move in with him. She could only imagine what his parents would think of the whole thing, despite the fact that she was one of Finn's friends and Aidan was a smart enough man to not be taken advantage of. Whenever there were massive amounts of money at stake, people grew wary and suspicious—and with just cause.

"What has you so nervous, love?" He glanced over at her before turning his attention back to the road. The plows had done a decent job of clearing the storm, and surprisingly enough, the temperature spiked to above freezing so the snow was now starting to melt.

The woods and fields around her had turned into a perfect winter wonderland, white and sparkly, like the world was covered in diamonds and everything was given a fresh start.

Aidan's SUV handled the snow with ease and he was a confident though careful driver. Not that she could blame him for being cautious, given his past.

"I'm still not sure I should be coming with you. And *please*, whatever you do, do *not* tell them that I'm moving in with you." This could be a disaster. Then they'd definitely think she was just trying to get her claws into him.

"You're worrying far too much about this. They're going to be ecstatic to see us, and if you think they won't realize you're a big part of getting me out of the house and over there, then you're mistaken. They're good judges of character, and they're going to love you." He gave her a sideways grin that made her heart melt, though she still wasn't sure.

"What if…" She let out a weary sigh, and tried to keep her heart from aching. "What if they're disappointed that you're with me?"

His jaw tensed and his knuckles went white around the steering wheel. "No one in their right mind could be disappointed in you. Do you hear me? It's time someone appreciated you for all you are—because you're damn special, Chloe, and I won't have anyone treating you otherwise. I'm telling you now—if anyone treats you with anything less than the respect you deserve, they'll be answering to me. Are we clear?"

All she could do is nod, though her heart swelled with love to know he cared enough to get upset on her behalf.

"We're here, love." He pulled the truck down a long drive to a pretty red farmhouse, decorated with pine swags at the windows and a wreath made of cranberries hanging on the front door. Against the backdrop of pristine snow, and with a lit Christmas tree in the large mullioned windows, she couldn't have picked a more perfect image.

"It's gorgeous, Aidan." Nothing extravagant, but nicely done, and quintessential New England.

With the car parked, he turned towards her and cupped the back of her neck with his large hand and pulled her in close for a sweet kiss, his stubble ticklish against her skin. "They're going to love you, sweetheart. Are you ready?"

With him at her side, she just might be ready for anything. And the way he looked at her, as if she were perfect, as if there was no one else there but the two of them…She felt her heart fall completely head over heels in love with him, her heart beating a staccato against her chest. "You make me believe anything's possible. So…yeah. I think I am ready."

He took her hand as they wandered up the path to the front door, her shoulders and gut in knots from the adrenaline coursing through her. And though he seemed relaxed, she, too, could sense the tension in him. This couldn't be easy for him either.

He didn't bother to knock, but rather let them in, leading the way as they stepped into the living room where everyone was gathered. He gave them a shy smile that made her want to hug him and secured the hold he had on her heart. "Don't suppose you have room for two more?"

The room around them erupted with surprise and happiness as his family rushed forward to greet them. Aidan hugged his father and then his mother, who already had tears in her eyes, before shaking hands and hugging a dozen other people—aunts, uncles, and cousins by the look of it. Chloe did her best to step to the side so they could have their time together without her getting in the way, though it wasn't long before Aidan was reaching back for her hand.

He pulled her close with a reassuring smile, even as her heart threatened to beat out of her chest, not sure his parents would be too keen on having an intruder interrupt the moment. "This here is Chloe. She's a college friend of Finn's…and quite special to me."

She must have blushed a dozen shades of red at his words. She shook his father's hand and was then pulled into a hug by his mom, when Finn walked into the room, his long gait only adding to his laid-back charm. He looked so much like Aidan with his handsome good looks—though Finn was clean-shaven, his hair was more tousled and a shade lighter, and he wore a grin that always spelled trouble.

"No way! Chloe—what the hell are you doing here, girl?" He pulled her into a hug that had her feet dangling a foot in the air.

"I got trapped on Mermaid Isle during the storm, and Aidan was nice enough to let me weather out the storm with him." It was the truth, even though there was a bit more to their story. Still, she didn't think she needed to spell things out for the group assembled when they'd walked in, hand in hand.

His mother gave her a genuine smile that was filled with so much emotion. "Well, we're so glad Aidan brought you along. Just in time, too—we're just getting ready to eat."

Finn hung an arm around his brother's shoulder. "And the ham is damn good—bourbon and brown sugar-glazed—though I swear, if there's any missing, it wasn't me."

Aidan shook his head with a smile that had Chloe's heart skipping a beat. "It'll be a miracle if there's any food left at all if no one stopped you from wandering into the kitchen."

She loved the banter between them, especially since it reminded her so much of her own brothers. She'd have to call home. Maybe go and visit once she knew the roads were clear.

Standing by the Christmas tree, the lights sparkled as the heady scent of pine filled her head. Aidan pulled her into his arms and kissed the top of her head, and though they were off in a corner on their own, she couldn't help but feel like their hug hadn't gone unnoticed.

Settling against his chest, he bowed his head to hers as her heartbeat picked up his rhythm so they beat as one. "Chloe…I hope you know how much you mean to me. And it goes beyond giving me my life back. I look at you, and I can't believe how lucky I am."

"I think we're both pretty damn lucky, Aidan. You've made me realize that I can't second-guess myself, and guilt has no place when it comes to making decisions that affect my life." It'd been hard for her to come to that realization, but she felt at peace for the first time in a very long time.

"I couldn't have said it any better myself." He gave her a sweet kiss that made her forget it wasn't just the two of them. "I love you, Chloe. As crazy as that may sound. But I swear it's true. I love you with all my heart."

Her heart swelled with such joy and love for him, it ached. "I believe you, Aidan, because I swear, I love you too."

He cupped her face in his large hand, and looked at her with eyes she'd never tire of losing herself in. "I'm hands down the luckiest man. Merry Christmas, love."

She stole just one more kiss, thinking that he wasn't the only one luck had smiled upon. "Merry Christmas to you too, love."

~The End~

Other Books In The Mermaid Isle Series:
One Sweet Summer
For Love Or Treasure

Made in the USA
San Bernardino, CA
22 January 2014